WELCOME TO THE WHISKEY REBELLION

"Good afternoon, Postman. And what tidings bring you from Pittsburgh Town?"

"None so diverting as to occasion a delay in the United States Mail, Mr. Highwayman."

The thief sighed. "Give your pouch to me, rider, and be on your way. Tell the authorities it was Tom the Tinker's men relieved you of your burden."

The postal rider sat and thought it over. Then resignedly turned in his saddle, reeled in the spare mount, and stretched for the mail pouch.

And turned around again with metal glinting in his fist.

Craaack!

An intense beam of emerald, bright and solid as if made of glass, spiked toward the thief.

There was an explosion of scarlet mist...

Also by L. Neil Smith

Published by Ballantine Books:

THE GALLATIN DIVERGENCE

L. NEIL SMITH

A Del Rey Book
BALLANTINE BOOKS • NEW YORK

A Del Rey Book
Published by Ballantine Books

Copyright © 1985 by L. Neil Smith

Library of Congress Catalog Card Number: 85-90720

ISBN 0-345-30383-0

Manufactured in the United States of America

First Edition: September 1985

Cover Art by Rick Sternbach

DEDICATED

to the memory of Gordon Kahl

ACKNOWLEDGMENT: for the kindly advice of Loise R. White of Brownsville, Pennsylvania, her son, Rick White, Dr. Jim Hansen, and the efforts of Leland D. Baldwin, author of *Whiskey Rebels* (University of Pittsburgh Press, 1968), my grateful thanks. If, in embellishing the events of 1794, I have unwittingly injured the shades of John Baldwin, John Holcroft, David Bradford, Benjamin Parkinson, or any of their associates, I tender my posthumous regrets. To Hugh Henry Brackenridge, John Neville, or Alexander Hamilton, I offer no apologies whatever.

Contents

"Should an attempt be made to suppress these people, I am afraid the question will not be, whether you will march to Pittsburgh, but whether they will march to Philadelphia, accumulating in their course, and swelling over the banks of the Susquehanna like a torrent..."

—Hugh Henry Brackenridge, in a letter to Tench Coxe, August, 1794

Is It Soup, Yet?

SOMEWHAT LATER...

"Lips!"

I shook my head, trying to focus on the blurry but familiar figure before me.

It was small, not much over five metric feet, scented with lavender, maybe ninety-five pounds, soaking wet—not counting the .50-caliber pistol certain to be belted around its waist. It had come from San Antonio—born in the shadow of an Alamo where the Texans had beaten Santa Anna—but acquired a certain polish, a certain *elan vital* in such disparate locales as Kansas, Prussia, Antarctica, and Ceres Central, principal metropolis of the Natural Asteroids.

And it was thoroughly, *gloriously* pissed off.

For me, it was like peering through a steamy windowpane. Letting a groan escape, I dragged my legs over the edge of the couch, levered myself upright, planted my dogs on the floor. The ants were having a square dance on the soles of my feet. I gave my scalp a thorough going-over, then fisted my eyelids. Phosphenes danced in the corners of my field of vision.

"Run that by me again, Lucy? I'm a little slow, this century."

"*Lips* I said, an' *Lips* I meant! Hot patootie, Winnie, we hadn't even got to the weddin' scene, when a coupla goons from Griswold's come an' hauled me right outa the late night double feature, water pistol, Zwieback, flashlight, bagga rice, an' all! I thought they was ushers, crackin' down on contraband, else I woulda plugged 'em right where they was Velcroed to!"

Griswold's. The oldest—and toughest—security outfit in the Confederacy. The grim, textured tartan they wore was black on black, and they carried more iron than Lucy did. Their motto wasn't *quite* "No Quarter;" it just seemed that way, sometimes.

Brrr.

I squeezed my eyelids shut until tears rimmed the lashes, blinked a time or two . . . *and I could see*. And I wished I couldn't.

Lucille Gallegos Kropotkin stood before me, gray-shot hair combed into a crazy-crinkled Afro, decorated with what looked for all the world like chicken bones. She'd painted circles under her eyes, makeup slashing down to the jawline. Her lips were colored white, her teeth stained red. She wore fishnet stockings, a lacy garter belt, a black Merry Widow accented with tiny scarlet bows that looked downright ridiculous on a little old lady her apparent age. Her spiked heels looked even sillier in our local twentieth of a gravity. A threadbare feather boa was draped around her scrawny shoulders . . . and, yes, the heavy Gabbet Fairfax automatic I'd anticipated, knobby, knurled, menacing, hung in a broad plastic gunbelt slanted around her skinny waist.

Were the tips of my fingers tinged with blue, or was it just imagination?

"Lucy, whether Clarissa's cured or not, I'm going back to sleep until women's styles change again!" Suppressing a yawn, I added, "What the hell year is this, anyway?"

"343, sleepyhead, *Anno Liberatis*—A.D. 2119, in case you're still mother-tongue groggy—Saturday, October thirteenth, an' later'n y'think, like always." Under the heavy makeup, her expression changed, from the high dudgeon she'd been enjoying, to a grave aspect I hadn't seen much over the years—centuries, now—I'd known her.

"Lucy, what's the matter? Is it—" A chill swept through me that had nothing to do with the stasis I'd been suspended in for, let's see . . . forty-four years. I remembered: there was a small percentage of mortality involved that— "Is it *Clarissa*?"

"Naw, she's fine. Still nappin', right beside where you been makin' zees all this time." She cleared her throat, stood straighter, wrapping an invisible cloak of dignity about herself. "Winnie, I gotta get this part over with now: Clarissa is *not* cured."

Something with big, cold hands wrapped its fingers around my stomach and *squeezed*. "What? Then why—"

"On account of I took it on m'self t'authorize wakin'
you. Wouldn't blame you if you punched me in the
nose—or rolled over an' went back t'sleep." She
inhaled, let it out through her nose, slapped a skinny
fist into a palm. "Plain truth is, we're in a bad place,
an' we needya."

"Nice to be indispensable," I grunted, looking around
me. It was the same hospital-style preparation room,
all right. Exactly. A big picture window in a stained
plastic setting displayed a sunlit meadow back on Earth.
Probably a subdivision by now—or a graveyard. The
overplush carpeting still rolled across the floor right
up the wall opposite the walk-in fireplace, with its four-
foot andirons in the disarmed shape of Venus de Milo.
There were deep-cushioned peacock chairs around a
table that would have suited Henry VIII—or the Har-
lem Globetrotters—and a Cleopatrine velvet sofa I was
half sitting, half lying on. Like the admiral said to the
duchess, anything worth doing is worth *over*doing.

I was dressed, just as I'd been . . . before. And there
was still no cure for Koman's Mitochondriasis. Four
and a half decades gone, with nothing to show for it
except Lucy's graying hair? Fighting the curtain of
dread I felt descending, I rubbed a hand across my still
numb face. "All right," I asked. "Who's '*we're*'?"

She hitched at her girdle, parked herself on the sofa
beside me. "The Confederacy, of course. The Solar
System. The Known Galaxy. Everybody, Win, everybody there *is*. Everybody there was or ever *will* be.
Whatcha want, hero, egg in your beer?"

"Aha! *Win Bear Saves The Universe!* It's a *dream*,

a goddam—" I paused in mid-thought. "Gee, I didn't know you could dream in stasis."

Lucy sighed, reached over, flicked the blue-enameled nail of her right index finger against the end of my nose. It hurt.

"Your brainpan's *still* frozen, Winnie! This ain't no dream, though I wish t'Lysander it was! Mebbe I oughta wish to Albert Gallatin; it'd be a passle more appropriate!"

Albert Gallatin had been the founder, in 1794—C.E.— of what was later to become the North American Confederacy. In the portion of reality *I'd* come from, the United States of America, he'd settled for Secretary of the Treasury in Thomas Jefferson's cabinet. Historically, it had made all the difference between the two universes. But what did that have to do with anything? For perhaps the hundred-thousandth time since I'd first met her one sunny bullet-pocked afternoon in 1987, I growled, "What the hell are you talking about, Lucy?"

"Parajective reality, Winnie—or was it *meta*jective reality? They didn't gimme time to get that part straight."

There was a moment of silence. Then she looked up at me. "Ooloorie had me arrested, shoved a quick briefin' down m'throat while you were thawin', an' I hustled out here, *prontissimo*. Total elapsed time, from Tim Curry to you—an' no improvement, I hope t'shout—twenty-three minutes flat!"

"Twenty-three *minutes*? Lucy, there isn't another asteroid within two *hours* of this one."

A *long* moment of silence this time.

Then I nodded. "Forty-four years. There have been improvements in transportation, haven't there?" Too bad there hadn't been in medicine.

She grinned, warming to a subject dear to whatever she was using for a heart these 'days, Progress. "You can say *that* again, with afterburners! Kiddo, it's gettin' so a body don't have any privacy at all! Time for movin' on . . ." She braked to an abrupt halt. "Only we got this little problem, first."

"Problem?" The woman I loved was dying by inches—make that molecules—and Lucille Gallegos Kropotkin, a little old lady who'd make Pearson and Shaw sorry they'd been right, said *she* had a problem.

"It's them Hamiltonians, Winnie."

"Hamiltonians?"

Lucy's scowl would have soured nondairy creamer. "Guess I'd better tellya where we stand: there've been improvements in all *kindsa* transporation. Now one of them authoritarian varmints's traveled back in *time*—

"—to assassinate Albert Gallatin!"

2

Clarissa Bear, Deceased

SOMEWHEN EARLIER...

It was cold.

They'd promised it wouldn't be. They'd explained how ambient temperature hadn't anything to do with it. They'd pointed out the warm browns, oranges, yellows of the decor, the crackling holo of a fireplace, just like we had at home—setting aside those andirons. They'd even mentioned the unmentionable (seeing I was a Healer's husband), that the process just *began* here. We were headed for colder storage, wouldn't be conscious to appreciate what they avoided calling our final resting place.

But it was *cold*.

I stubbed my last cigar out, lay down on a preparation-table disguised as a studio couch, ignoring the indoctrination coming from the Telecom across the room, just as I ignored the phony fireplace, the phony picture window, the shaggy wallpaper. Instead, I focused on Clarissa, the Light of my Life, the Mother of my Children, the Moon of my Desire—the little girl I'd sentenced to a grisly death.

MONDAY, JUNE 10, 299 A.L.

"Koman's viroid," Clarissa had intoned with unnatural evenness. She called up a display from the neutrinomicroscope I'd given her last Painemas. I would have guessed viruses are round or cylindrical, simpler than bacteria. This thing looked like a pair of Groucho Marx nose-glasses. Ignominious, being done in by a dimestore novelty.

"One hundred percent fatal," she continued, "noncontagious, rare in the Confederacy." Her chin began quivering as she shifted from detached professional to future statistic.

"*But not rare enough!*" I roared. "Damn it, how could this have *happened* to us?" I guess I'd always thought of her as indestructible. Plenty of bad actors had tried for a piece of both of us—and wound up with bloodied noses. Now, tangling with a micronemesis that made a pinpoint resemble Mount Everest, I was learning differently. I shook the feeling of futility settling over me like a weighted net. *Damn*, there were things I knew she wanted to do! Now they'd have to be postponed. Forever.

This much I could help her with: "Arrangements" have to be made in a hurry when a disease even the North American Confederacy can't cure rips through your body like a prairie fire. Funny how habits of language linger on. They hadn't called it *North American* for a long time. It was the *Solar* Confederacy now, on its way to becoming the *Galactic* Confederacy. And I hadn't seen a prairie (let alone that kind of fire) in half a century.

I shook my head. My mind was wandering, but it was too weak to get very far. Not feeling much of anything, I chucked the 'Com pad we'd been looking at, a hand-held terminal linked to the household retrieval system (including Clarissa's microscope) onto her desk in the office/surgery we called her Sewing Room, and sat down in the desk chair.

The place was a sterile, pastel green, lined with racks of instruments and supplies, yet feminine, imprinted with her personality—despite the odor of disinfectant that seems as ritually necessary as incense in a Buddhist temple. "Not 'how', sweetheart," I answered my own rhetorical complaint, "but *where*? Courtesy of good old Laporte Interworld Terminal."

I grunted. The cynics were right, no good deed goes unpunished. This Koman gink had been a Broach-explorer. Some folks were content traveling between *known* worlds, studying divergent civilizations, smuggling forbidden fruit, fomenting an occasional revolution. This clown had poked around for *new* realities, cultures contemporary to our own, but with different histories, different triumphs and disasters...

The P'wheet-Thorens Probability Broach had been discovered (that's the word: they'd been trying to *invent* a star-drive) in 194 A.L. Make that A.D. 1970 for people unused to doing their calendric reckoning in terms of the American Revolution. I'd come from such a place, a depression-battered United States of America, but was "collected" by Ooloorie Eckickeck P'wheet, during early live-sample experiments. I'd been a homicide detective for the City and County of Denver.

My name's Win Bear.

1987 had been a bad year for wine and everything else, unemployment and inflation well into double digits and trying for three. It was a toss-up whether we were going to die first from pollution or starvation. Everything was scarce, everything rationed, especially freedom. And make that 211 A.L., for people and places unused to the assumption that everybody ought to have the same religion. Or any religion at all.

The Confederacy had been such a place, the result of the Pennsylvania Whiskey Rebellion's having turned out differently—thanks to Albert Gallatin. Back home, it was the first occasion that the central government (located in Philadelphia at the time) tried collecting taxes, under President George Washington, Treasury-Secretary Alexander Hamilton, and a brand-new Federalist Constitution. The taxees, between sessions with hot tar and feathers reserved for Hamilton's collectors, had wanted to know why they'd bothered to duke it out with England a generation earlier. There'd almost been a second Revolution.

Here in the Confederacy, carrying their tar and feathers from Pittsburgh to the City of Brotherly Love, the second-revolutionaries had won. Washington had exhaled the smoke of his final cigarette through a dozen bullet holes. Hamilton had found the slug with *his* name on it in Prussia—where he'd bugged out to—rather than at the trigger-finger of Aaron Burr.

Koman's World (as it came to be called, just before they sealed it off forever) was *another* alternative—from an available infinity—and not the only one where humankind had finished the job of destroying themselves. There were hundreds of cindered, radioactive Earths, places where the planet was reduced to cosmic gravel, and some where man-made—rather, *government*-made—diseases had done the dirty work.

Koman's World was the worst of a bad lot. The trouble there was that they hadn't *quite* finished. Clarissa had responded, with a dozen other Healers, to a call from the original explorers. Naturally, I went along. The call took us to Newfoundland, Belle Isle, about twenty miles from where the city of St. John's had been, the only place on the planet where something resembling human life remained—a hundred pitiable specimens who might have been native Newfies, descendants of Canadian troops, Americans, even Russians. They wouldn't talk to us, except to call themselves "The Winners." Even willing, they weren't in any shape to tell us more than that.

I'd always thought they failed to trust us because we came in spacesuits. And never took them off. One by one "The Winners" succumbed. There wasn't anything we could do except commit their bodies to the leaden waters of Conception Bay, contemplating what a swell incentive a worldwide antinuclear treaty had provided for the development of biological warfare.

We burned our spacesuits afterward.

*   *   *

"I can tell you what it *is*." She knelt beside the chair, where I focused on the wall across the surgery, ignoring the furniture's attempt to massage me into feeling better.

"Yeah?"

"A simplified virus, hovering at the edge of our best definitions of life—" She used the 'Com pad to call up microphotographs of the viroid "—designed to attack human mitochondria. Elegant engineering, in a horrible way, since mitochondria are foreign to the rest of the cell. There's some thought they were independent organisms, like chloroplasts in plant cells, even to possessing their own peculiar DNA complement."

Having been a murder cop has advantages. The peculiar DNA complement I call my own echoed her momentary objectivity. "Elegantly devastating, since without mitochondria, the body can't produce energy." I paused, gathering courage. "How much time left, honey?"

She looked away, her face contorted by the anguish we both felt. Big tears rolled down her cheeks, taking their languid time in the almost nonexistent gravity. She started to speak, couldn't make the words come out. What the hell, I wasn't in a hurry to hear them.

I hadn't expected her to live forever, but I'd grown accustomed to the science of my adopted culture, enough to feel cheated. I'd come here at the age of forty-eight, plagued with everything that implied in the twentieth-century U.S., plus ulcers, baldness, rotten teeth, chronic fatigue, incipient cancer, thrown in as a bonus for a lifetime of police work. Without government to stifle progress—it had never recovered from being forbidden to collect taxes—the Confederacy was way ahead, having found means to reverse the aging process. I'd even gotten back my hair and teeth.

Clarissa was every bit as beautiful as the day I'd met her, eighty-eight years before. She looked cute in her medical pastels, the ones with the circled white cross on the shoulder. I never thought admiring my wife would make me feel depressed. Thoughts going around inside my head had the acrid odor of cigarette smoke in a bathroom. "Three weeks," she told me at last, "perhaps a little less. Oh, Win, what are we—"

"Three weeks?" I'd known it was bad, but I was still surprised. "Some virus! And you say you're not contagious?"

Clarissa blinked. "Win, a thousand other Broach-explorers could have opened Koman's World in perfect safety. By mischance—fortunate, since the warning saved the lives of others—he had that rare suscepti-bility that..."

"That you seem to share."

"That I seem to share." She rose, crossed the room, began rearranging the supply shelves. We didn't say anything for a long while. I lit a cigar. "Well, at least I won't die of lung cancer, after you're gone." I fingered the big Smith & Wesson under my left armpit. "Will there be much pain?"

She whirled, scattering teardrops. "Cancer I could *cure*, blast all the luck! There *will* be pain...but I can deal with that." She watched me, aware of the way I was playing with the antique six-gun: "Dear, *please* don't do anything...well, *permanent*. Who knows, science might come up with an answer any—"

Shock hummed through my body. "Wait a minute, Clarissa, are you telling me that someday, some-body—"

She gave it professional consideration. "Research goes on all the time, darling. Slowly on a rare disease like this one." Her eyebrows lifted. "I don't know, it could be the making of some graduate student's—"

"Then the answer's simple." I stood up, pulled her close to me. "We'll *freeze* you."

She dropped her jaw, astonished she hadn't thought of it herself. She's sharp, but has her limits. Like thinking clearly when she's about to croak. I was excited. "We'll take everything we have, invest it at high interest until there's a big enough grant to *find* a cure."

She laughed, startled at my burst of pragmatism. "It isn't freezing, love. It's paratronic stasis, done at the subatomic level at room-temp—"

"I know all that. And I'm coming with you..."

"What?"

"That's right, we'll freeze me, too."

3
Rubble is My Business

At half a gravity's acceleration, it was four hours to Gary's Bait & Trust.

Clarissa and I had homesteaded that myriad of worldlets circumastrogating the Sun where a planet used to be. Venus hadn't been any great shakes as a world, but it made one hell of an asteroid belt. Our second daughter, EdWina, had been born out here. Both girls, she and Terra-born Lucille, had grown up with a constellation of pioneer values that sent them farther out as grownups to explore the stars.

Me, I was content exploring my own life.

Home turned out to be wherever Clarissa hung her diploma. Moving from Earth to "1939 Chandler" (the official designation of our planetoid), I'd set up as the Venus Belt's first private investigator. I can't swear I was the best P.I. the Confederacy ever had, but, even at civilization's fringes, there was always more work than I could handle. We were spared more traditional, callous-generating frontier pursuits like farming and mining.

Survey be damned, *we* called our asteroid "Little Sister"—partly after EdWina—and the home we built there, High Window. When enough sterile rock had been bacteriaformed into soil, our atmospheric envelope installed, and a hired engineer (L.G. Kropotkin) had declared we had—just—enough gravity to keep a decorative pond in place, I imitated another flatfoot from a favorite novel and had a replica constructed of Copenhagen's little mermaid. The women in my life dubbed her The Lady In The Lake. It had been a short life, but a brief one, and now, thanks to Koman's Mitochondriasis, we were headed for The Big Sleep.

Farewell, my lovelies.

Adoption of fictional names for asteroids wasn't an isolated lunacy, original with the Bears. Civilization, occupying Earth, Mars, Earth's moon, the Natural Asteroids (which had proven no more natural than the Bogus Belt we lived in), so many minor satellites I've lost track—*plus* the subdivison of all subdivisions we'd staked out a corner of . . . Well, our rapidly expanding civilization had long since run out of names for ancient gods. Even if it'd been inclined that way in the first place. On the other hand, every paperback novel, every C-minus movie and up, every memorable character created by Confederate yarn spinners of those of other universes (from which had come millions of refugees like myself) had its namesake amid the rocks, rocklets, and rockettes we humans, porpoises, gorillas, chimps, and I don't know what-all-else called home.

Gary's Bait & Trust was the closest thing our stretch offered to a hospital. Begun as a tackle shop for folks with backyard fishing-holes, the sizable stasis-locker for bait promised other lucrative possibilities. Oh, Gary's was a real bank by now, with tellers' cages, proof machines, and friendly, friendly loan officers. It was still a legitimate bait shop, too. It was also where you kept an extra pancreas if you'd thought to have one cloned, or withdrew a pair of corneas if you were hard up for same, and therefore a natural place to make our own "deposit."

We parked our Buick Beltmaster in the puddle of chewing gum serving as a landing-port on 2323 Goldfinger (*also* not the official survey name and number). The asteroid's gravity was a puny twentieth of standard, the sticky paving an absolute necessity. The old-fashioned flivver, one of a great variety of personal craft that were automobiles for gravity-free portions of the Confederacy, would find its own way back to Little Sister.

That we'd closed up for the vacuum-packed duration, six months or six thousand years. Putting ourselves in escrow had required several days and all the computer-capacity we possessed. We both had clients to refer to other practitioners. There were messages to record for our daughters aboard the giant star-saucer *Tom Paine Maru*, light-years beyond immediate reach. There were also friends to see.

Like Ed and Lucy.

* * *

"Koman's *what*?"

Edward William Bear—not me, but somebody else—sat in the other half of the prep-room, protected by a pane of talented Confederate glass. Clarissa may not have been contagious, but it never hurts to take precautions.

In his case, I wasn't really worried. You see, Ed has my genes. Also my taste in cigarettes and liquor, my choice of professions, many of my personal habits and mannerisms—and my fingerprints. He wasn't my twin—even identicals are supposed to have different prints—nor was he my clone. In fact, he didn't bear any blood-relationship to me at all—except that he was my type, RH-factor, and HLA pattern. If we'd dressed at all alike (I'd spent too many decades as a U.S. cop for that to be much of a possibility in the flamboyant Confederacy—and white socks are *comfortable*, damn it!), the only two individuals who might have told us apart were my wife the Doctor, and Lucy the . . . the Whatever-she-was. And I'm not even sure about Lucy.

But then I never am.

Somewhere there's a universe where Napoleon won the Battle of Waterloo. That world and our own (whichever you care to hang your hat in) were each supplied with its own personal Napoleon—there have been exactly as many Napoleons as universes in which he appeared. Circular, I know, but things work out that way in real life.

In 1815 (or 39 A.L.), when Napoleon was *losing* his final battle in the pair of universes I know about, James Madison was President of the United States. So was

Monsieur Citizen Edmond Genet, immigrant successor to Albert Gallatin—of the *Old* United States, which evolved into the North American Confederacy.

In 1939 (163 A.L.), when Adolf Schicklegruber was applying his John Hancock to a highly disposable Non-Aggression Pact with Joseph Djugashvili (and their counterparts were out looking for honest jobs in *this* universe-next-door), my favorite author was writing his first—and best—book in the U.S.A. In the North American Confederacy the "same" guy was collaborating with a fellow named Hammett on their master-piece-built-for-two, *Night Domain*. Remember, the one they made a classic holo of, during the War against the Czar in 1957?

Also, on the twelfth of May, Edward William Bear was born in Denver, Colorado, U.S.A.—at the same time he was being born in St. Charles-Auraria, N.A.C.

The St. Charles-Aurarian Bear leaned back, smoked his cigar, and stared at me through the glass. The stuff was strong—grenade-proof—elastic as a rubber sheet. It could have been a mirror if he hadn't insisted on adjusting the pattern of his clothing to a flowery Hawaiioid design I had trouble prying my horrified eyes from. Lime green on fluorescent pink will do that to you.

"So you'll wind up younger than I am." He observed. "If it takes ten years to find a cure, when they wake you up, I'll have aged a decade, and you won't."

I shook my head. "Some difference that'll make. Look at us now, both over a century old, and—"

"An' *babies*, compared to some of us!" Lucy Kropotkin, Ed's wife and—literally—my oldest friend, snorted, took a drag on her own cigar, blew a ring, and poked her finger through it. Currently young and attractive, she perched on his chair-arm, one foot on the seat beside Ed's thigh, a hand spread on her hip like a rubber-suited George Sand. If George Sand had been inclined to yellow paisley. "I'm pushin' two hundred an' a quarter, an' I expect t'be around to help 'em thaw you kids out, if it takes eleventy-million years! Never had a sick day in my life," she lied—she'd been recovering from industrial-grade radiation-poisoning when I'd first met her. "Never had time t'spare!"

Born in 75 A.L. (A.D. 1851), Lucy had already enjoyed several colorful lifetimes, enough for any *five* mortals. She'd spent plenty of effort making them even more colorful for the benefit of any poor devil unable to pry her fingers from his lapels and run for earplugs. Married more times than she could keep track of, mostly to adventurous younger men she'd outlived, she was an engineer, a lawyer of sorts, the closest thing the Confederacy had to a politician, and, at least according to her, had once—by a desperate last-minute maneuver—narrowly missed being elected President.

Most individuals chose, under the life-extending regimen of Confederate geriatrics, to look the same age all the time. I favored the apparent mid-forties—good for business. Lucy liked to rejuvenate radically, age into her elderly aspect, then rejuvenate all over again, claiming it gave her a broader perspective on the human condition. At present, she looked eighteen, not beautiful, but all dark eyes and raven hair. It was only in the decade following regained youth that she showed her Mexican ancestry. Most of the time she seemed like somebody's—everybody's—little old grandmother. That is, if everybody's little old grandmother smoked cigars and carried a .50-caliber automatic pistol. I believe even Ed preferred her that way. Thinking about it, so did I.

Clarissa (who maintained her age at thirty) stood behind me, hands on the back of my chair, addressing Lucy through the glass. "And we'll both be happy to see you, dear, though I *hope* it isn't any million years. Our contract with the real-estate managers doesn't run that long, and it would take *another* million just to catch up on my journals!"

"Which risk *we* aren't in danger of," Ed observed. He flicked his cigar ashes in the general direction of the suction-tray on the other arm of his chair. And missed. "I'll bet detectiving wasn't much different in Neanderthal times. Better information technology now, scientific criminology and all that, but—"

"But—" I agreed. "—there was still some poor schmuck in a leopard-skin trenchcoat standing in a rainy cave-entrance to keep an eye on Mrs. Ungh and her boyfriend on behalf of Mr. Ungh?"

"I don't take divorce work," Ed replied.

"I do; I need the money." Or would have, if Confederate divorce weren't a matter of go away, you bother me. "Anyway, it was nice of you two, coming all the way from Triton to see us off. What're you planning for your *own* next few centuries?"

"Nothin' spectacular," Lucy answered. "They're

openin' up some promisin' rocks out Cometary way, beyond Pluto. Gettin' hard t'keep up: some entrepreneur name of Wilson's offerin' two good-sized semi-planets called Mickey an' Goofy, but we prefer t'do our pioneerin' on our own. Shucks, we ain't even done settlin' *this* system yet, already they're startin' on the rest of the galaxy! We might just save up our boxtops, get ourselves a secondhand starship!—" She steered her cigar through the air, made a rude noise involving lips and tongue that sounded more like a motorcycle in need of a tune-up than a faster-than-light drive. "We'll keep tracka things, though, an' be back when they wake you. That's a promise!"

We both nodded, Clarissa blinking back tears.

So now it was The Long Good-bye.

They'd started Clarissa early, something about her illness. Maybe she'd wanted to slip into something more comfortable. It's nobody's business what we found to say, our last few hours together. When they thawed me out, however many eons from now, I'd *still* be chafed in certain embarrassing places. At least she'd be in the ice-cube tray next to mine. We'd wanted something cozier, but they haven't gotten around to Eternal Double Occupancy yet at Gary's Bait & Trust. Bankers are so conservative.

There was a thrumming in the air. The room seemed colder than before. I hoped I hadn't left the bathtub running back home.

Maybe by the time they woke us, places like this would have mirrored ceilings. Heart-shaped pools.

Closed-circuit superconducting porno. Infinite Kink. Wouldn't be surprised at all.

The lights grew dimmer.

I sure wished I'd had time to smoke one final...

4

Coffee and Pistols

SATURDAY, OCTOBER 13, 343 A.L.

Lucy opened her mouth to continue. The Telecom war-
bled. A wall lit with the image of a reception desk,
where a female chimp sat filing her nails. Under "A"
for "Ancient Bad Joke."

"*Mr. Bear, you've another caller. Shall I tell her
not to bother you?*"

Lucy waved me off before I could answer. "Cue her
up, honey—an' tell her she owes me a bagga popcorn!"

The 'Com dissolved to an untidy laboratory full of
complicated apparatus, its central feature a shiny
wheeled contraption supporting nine feet of *Tursiops
truncatus*—Latin for turkey of the sea. Ooloorie Eckickeck P'wheet reposed before us, in a vehicle better-
suited to the five-day racetrack than a physics lab.

"Lucille Gallegos Kropotkin, it is gratifying to hear
your voice again. We lacked time for a proper greeting

before. Edward William Bear..." She gave a second glance Lucy's way, took in the corset, the makeup, the chicken bones, the stockings. "Oh. Is that still playing out there?"

Ooloorie was the dolphin half of the P'wheet/Thorens Broach-inventing ensemble, specializing in esoteric math. Her sidekick, Deejay, who'd actually constructed the abomination, had long since emigrated starward. Last time I'd had the dubious pleasure of conversing with the porpoise, she'd been 'Comming from her split-level aquarium at San Francisco's Emperor Norton University—though she'd been known to travel, even out to Venus once, just in time to supervise the planet's catastrophic renovation. It made a certain demented sense that the cetacean Einstein would be involved up to her streamlined appendages in anything connected with time-travel. Hopping from world to alternate world was the same idea, after all, only sideways. But how did that concern Lucy—and a defective detective who'd turned himself into a popsicle so he could spend the rest of oblivion with his daughters' momsicle?

"Hello, Ooloorie," I answered. "Invent anything new and dangerous lately?"

Behind the dolphin's deceptively heiferlike eyes, back of the smooth curve of her forehead, percolated more raw intelligence than I'd used all my life—but could she cook? Her permanent grin was as deceptive as the placid eyes. "Landling, there is nothing worth inventing that is not inherently dangerous. I have invented many things since last I saw you—it has been decades for most of us, you realize. We lack time now for your habitual jocularity. Has Lucille Gallegos Kropotkin explained what has transpired?"

"Does she ever?"

That earned me a dirty look. "Hold on there, varmints! I was just about to, when you popped up, honey. Now you're available, why don'tcha take over? It'll fill in some gaps for me, too."

The scientist looked around the preparation room, activated her bike, and rolled right out of what I'd taken for a Telecom screen. She gave a shiver, wiggling end to end. "Is it not cold in here?"

"Not according to the tourist brochures. Lucy, where's a 'Com pad? Get them to turn up the thermostat. And promote us some coffee and tobacco. Especially tobacco!"

She reached a couple of fingers down her corset, extracted a pair of cigars, handed one to me. "Don't need 'Com pads any more, Winnie. Hey, Telecom!" The wall—I think it was a wall—lit up again.

The simian receptionist had finished her fingernails and begun on her toes. She looked up, annoyed at the interruption. *"May I help you?"*

"Yeah, honey, breakfast an' coffee for..." She examined me, came to the conclusion I was emaciated. "...make it five. An' stoke up the furnace? Colder'n a Siberian's sit-down in here!"

The nail file froze in mid-stroke *"Madame,"* protested the chimp, *"I assure you—"*

"Don't you *dast* call me 'madame' when I'm dressed like this! Just mind your programmin', rustle us up some grub, *muy schnell*—an' do somethin' about the heat 'fore I set fire to the furniture, get me?"

The room began to warm up.

Moments later, the "door" opened again, to a restaurant-kitchen background. A serving table enameled fire-engine red wafted in on a cushion of air. *"Break-fast for five?"* A snotty tone emanated from a jointed periscope at one end. *"But there are only* three *sapients here. Someone must have misprogrammed—"* Servos whining, it turned back to the door.

"Hold it, Boris Cartoff!" Lucy popped to her feet, one hand slapping at her holster. "If there's anything gets my goat worse'n uppity machinery— Bring them goodies back or you'll be routin' city sewage out Goofopolis way!"

The cart halted, turned, called her bluff. *"Do you imagine I* enjoy *being a waiter? It is of little interest to me, madame—"*

"There he goes agin!" Lucy protested. She turned to me. "I *gotta* change outa these duds. Everbody thinks I'm a—"

"Lucy," I interrupted, *"please* sit down and let Ooloorie tell us what's going on?" I looked at the cold cigar in my hand. "And give me a light, will you?"

Seeing its chance, the table lashed out a wiry chromium tentacle; the tip burst into flame. *"Light, sir?"*

"Just unload breakfast, and skip the apple-polishing. I've got half a century's eating to catch up on."

"Yes, sir."

"And don't stand there waiting for a tip. All my assets are frozen."

"That was funny, sir, the first *thousand times I heard it."*

"LUCY!"

"Toldya so, Winnie!" She drew her Gabbet Fairfax—the big long-recoil automatic looked like a section of railroad iron—thumbed the hammer back with a *clank*. The machine squeaked, slammed our breakfast down on the coffee table, then vanished, taking the door—or at least the view it gave us—with it.

Ooloorie sat watching all of this with the characteristic impatience she showed all landdwellers. She rolled her carriage forward a pace, rolled it back, then, with exasperation in her tone, asked, "Edward William Bear, do you remember the human, Hirnschlag von Ochskahrt?"

"Nope—hmmm..." I raised the cover on a steaming plate of green chili. Cubes of overcooked pork swam in spicy gravy. Breakfast didn't seem to have changed much in forty-four years. "What kind of oxcart was he?" In my racket, a memory for names and faces is the most important capital asset. If I didn't recall this guy of Ooloorie's—and I didn't—he'd never been consequential, to me or any of my clients.

"Ochskahrt." She spelled it. "An assistant of ours ...better than a century ago. Little wonder you do not remember him, he was a rather odd, anonymous wight, bald, thick exterior spectacles—"

I grinned. "And a head shaped like a light bulb?" I'd only met the subject on the 'Com, but hairlessness and eyeglasses were hens' teeth in the Confederacy. Rarer, when the advent of gene-tailoring made hens' teeth a salable novelty. Balditude was usually the result of some intractable psychological malady. So you could *still* blame it on your mother. "The singular affair of the disappearing flying saucer, wasn't it?" I referred to a case in the 1990s in which Ooloorie had proved helpful.

"That is the one. I had not heard from Hirnschlag von Ochskahrt for decades. He was . . . well, a little *clumsy*, a bad thing in an experimental laboratory. I was just as pleased when he resigned to go into business for himself."

"Doing what? There isn't much demand for a professional klutz." I opened the end of a baggie of orange juice, squeezed out a sip.

She shook her head. "As a custom inventor, operating out of Laporte. That is what he was doing when he was commissioned to invent a time-machine."

I'd heard the words already. I refrained from dropping the baggie, concentrated instead on forking a breakfast steak, three eggs, and six waffles out of the serving pieces and underneath the retaining cover of my own plate. Lucy started similar loading operations.

Ooloorie continued: "A female human, unidentifiable from his rather vague description, asked him to do it. Something about her aroused his suspicions, even before what happened later. The possibility for time-travel has always been inherent in the physics of the Broach, of course. We learned a great deal more about it during your flying-saucer case. I have even . . . But there is no point going into that. In any case, Hirnschlag von Ochskahrt was a little desperate for clients, so he ignored his second thoughts until afterward."

"Afterward?" I echoed around a mouthful of hash-browns and sausage.

"When she left him manacled to a bench with twenty-three metric pounds of plastique on time-delay, ticking away next to his invention. By then he understood what she was and what she planned to do. If it had not been for a beaker of acid he had carelessly spilled on the bench that morning—I told you he was clumsy—he would never have gotten loose. His machine was destroyed. Almost paralyzed with panic, he contacted me, and—"

"You were out in San Francisco at the time?"

"Beta Centauri IV, actually, attending a colloquium of—"

"Good heavens! How recently did this—"

"Eight days ago."

I looked at Lucy. "There *have* been improvements in transportation!" She nodded, went on stuffing pancakes and red peppers into her face with an absorption that didn't altogether explain her uncharacteristic silence. I let it ride. "And what," I said, "do you want me to do about it?"

Instead of an answer, Ooloorie extended a mechanical arm from her silvery framework. Clutched in its three-fingered manipulator was a large coinlike object, bronze, from the shabby look of it, unusual in a culture that used platinum, gold, silver, and copper for money. She laid it with a dull clank beside my plate.

I stopped eating, started choking.

Forty-four years without a meal or not, *this* morning's appetite was gone. Lucy had to slap me on the back several times, getting makeup all over me in the process. It's one thing to *hear* the word "Hamiltonian." It's another to be handed their calling card with breakfast. I knew its type too well. "Lucy, they *are* Hamiltonians!"

"Toldya so, Winnie. You hadda see for yourself."
She turned to Ooloorie. "You want some of this chow,
honey, 'fore it disappears?" Ooloorie rolled forward,
found a plate of kippers, and began making up for my
abrupt lack of interest in food.

Like the legendary planet Basketball, the Confederacy's a peaceful place. I'd been hired more often
to find lost pets than to tackle something involving foul
play. Yet here it was: foul play made manifest. The
coin was blank on one side, excepting the Christian
Era date Confederate history associates with the "Constitution Conspiracy" that triggered the Whiskey
Rebellion, Hamilton and Washington's parchment *coup
d'etat* in 1789. The "heads" side was embossed with
the ominous Eye-In-The Pyramid any U.S. citizen
would recognize from a dollar bill, thirteen steps, just
like a gallows. More skullduggery had been accomplished in *both* universes under that logo than the Cosa
Nostra ever dreamed of.

Pretending a casualness I didn't feel, I flipped the
villainous token in the air, caught it in the same hand,
gave my fist a shake, and squeezed the coin, hard.
Maybe I was hoping it would disappear the way breakfast was doing. Despite the room temperature, Ooloorie shivered again as she rolled back from the table,
a pistol whining on its servos in a scabbard on the side
of her contraption.

Thanks to the thoughtfulness of Gary's Bait & Trust,
my own piece was where it had always been, tucked
away beneath my left armpit. I levered it out of the
spring-holster. I'd used other weapons from time to
time, but we'd been through a lot together, this battered

old Smith & Wesson .41 and me. The Model 58 Military and Police, its makers had called it a century and a half ago. No fancy rib or adjustable sights or any other nonsense.

We'd both changed over the centuries. Its barrel was cut back from the standard four inches to a hip-pocket three, with slots either side of the front sight to direct recoil-forces. No small consideration in the gravity-poor Belt. The hammer-spur was bobbed to avoid entangling alliances, and I'd had a broad, smooth trigger installed for double-action work. The grip was rounded to K-frame size, more comfortable in my stubby hands. The entire weapon, blue-black to begin with, patina-gray in later years, had been plated to resemble stainless steel. I hoped I wouldn't need it. That was a bad sign. Most of the hair-raising adventures in my life had begun with hoping I wouldn't need the Model 58.

"She left it with Hirnschlag von Ochskahrt." Ooloorie referred to the medallion, explaining with her blowhole while her mouth was busy with my breakfast. "And from what she told him, it appears she's planning to—"

"Assassinate Albert Gallatin?" I asked, holstering the magnum.

"You told him," Ooloorie said to Lucy.

The old lady folded skinny arms around her frail chest. "An' you accused me of never explainin' nothin'. Whatcha wanna do, save it as a Christmas surprise?" To me: "Winnie, if Gallatin gets knocked off 'fore he leads the Whiskey Boys to victory, ain't gonna be nothin' recognizable left. You wanna be here when

Clarissa wakes up. Okay, we been through a lot together, I'll give it to you straight: this is gonna be a dangerous stunt. Wouldya rather gamble *not* bein' here, in an attempt at savin' Albert Gallatin's imported hide—an' mebbe the whole Confederacy with it?"

I opened my mouth to speak, but didn't get the chance.

"Or go back t'bed an' wake up a hundred years from now, non-existent?"

5

Backing Lookward

LATER THAT SAME DAY...

For the first time in forty-four years, I got to my feet.

"Win," Ooloorie said, finishing off the final bit of herring—it was the first I could remember her using my first name. "There is something else you ought to know..."

Gary's Bait & Trust had done a good job. Not a stiff joint anywhere. I walked around, bounced on my arches. My feet still hurt. For an excop, that was normal. I turned to face the dolphin. "What's that?"

Her emptied plate had followed Lucy's and mine through a slot in the table. Now she hesitated. People seemed to be doing a lot of that. Lucy watched her, something in the old lady's eyes I didn't like the look of.

"Venusian orbit," observed the physicist, "is a hostile environment. Without adequate technology, we

34

would expire in seconds. The trust company, like everyone else out here, maintains air pressure, humidity, a tolerable light-level, and—"

"And the proper magnetic ambience," I finished the litany for her.

"So your bones won't creep away," Lucy added, "a molecule at a time." Rummaging in her décolletage, she produced another pair of cigars, handed one to me.

"Go on," I said, lighting up, "I know all that. You forgot the temperature—"

Lucy snorted, giving the 'Com wall a dirty look. "I reckon it wasn't Ooloorie who forgot!"

"Yes, the temperature. And they also—the trust company, I mean—maintain the . . . the milieu of contemporaneity." She stopped there, expecting me to say something.

"The who of *what*?"

She assumed an exasperated tone. "There is an anachronicity limit, landling, on each chamber in this establishment, set for the individual client when he awakens. In your case, nothing is obtrusive that wasn't invented before 299 A.L., when you went into stasis. It is one of the services they are supposed to provide. Look at your contract. Outside, change has accumulated geometrically. They are trying to protect you from the—"

I tried to speak.

Lucy held up a hand: "If Winnie survived bein' the first person squoze through a Broach, he can take a little progress. We ain't got time t'tickle him into the fourth century easy-like. Won't matter, once we're back in 1794. Shucks, now's m'chance t'scrag Al Hamilton himself, ten years aheada schedule."

"Lucy!" Ooloorie was shocked, and not by the future. "You cannot do that, any more than we can permit Albert Gallatin—"

"Yeah, I know." She sighed. "But I can *dream*, can't I?"

I shouldn't have been surprised. Hamilton's no name to conjure with in the Confederacy. You can get Eggs Benedict anywhere this side of reality, but nobody ever heard of a Brandy Alexander. The late founder of the Federalist Party and the National Debt just had sour luck where booze was concerned. Losing the Whiskey Rebellion, he refugeed out to Prussia, only to get shot by an obscure Polish nobleman named Coveleskie.

After whom they named a fine Confederate liqueur.

But his unsavory shade (Hamilton's, not Coveleskie's) marches on. Where I come from, Europeans call any powerful hunting rifle a "Vinchester." Here, anyone who thinks he knows better how to run your life than you do—Fascist, Communist, Republican—is considered a generic Hamiltonian, whatever the specific brand name of his justification.

I didn't know about these clients of Ochskahrt's, but I was better acquainted with the breed than I wanted to be. John Jay Madison, for instance, and his henchman, Hermann Kleingunther. Or Ab Cromney, the particularly evil Edna Janof, and her paramour, Norrit Gregamer. Voltaire Malaise, self-styled Voice of the Stars. Only a hasty selection of the miscreants I'd dealt with over the years, each one worse than the other, each one dead or MIA—a fair percentage by my own hand—excepting good old Freeman K. Bertram, who'd swapped sides just in time to save my favorite skin. The North American Confederacy, a society without war or crime, was also unusual in teaching its children to *appreciate* those virtues. Nonetheless, in every generation, even in this liberty-loving land, a small minority of defectives managed to crawl out from under their rocks and do their best, for a while, to make life difficult for the rest of us.

Until we were forced to make it impossible for them.

Afterward, we'd pass the box of Band-Aids, heave a big, ragged sigh of relief, and tell ourselves that, at long last, the Hamiltonian Society—or its current imitators—wouldn't trouble us anymore.

Ha.

I'd awakened wearing the rubbery silver all-purpose "smartsuit" of the third-century Confederacy, intended for the airless depths of space. It had proved itself in every other possible environment, and in time had become standard civilized apparel—like the gray flannel suit of 1950s America. Also standard was the lightweight cloak I wore, and the shoulder-holster underneath—though my ancient space-conditioned Smith & Wesson had received its share of peculiar stares from the first day I'd packed it in this universe of laser-pistols, miniature mass-accelerators, and plasma-squirting elephant-demolishers.

Now, Lucy sported her Happy Hooker outfit, Ooloorie her bicycle and a big grin—I wondered how she kept her skin damp, a vital necessity for her kind. The smartsuit, unlike the convention of personal armament, seemed to have fallen out of style in the shiny new fourth-century Confederacy. If we were headed for the eighteenth century, something would have to be done about appropriate costumes. In theory, Ed was off somewhere making arrangements. None of us took time to change now.

"I suppose—" The physicist nodded toward the door. "—we might as well get started." At least I think it was a door. Without further instruction, it redilated to the cluttered laboratory scene, and, with even less fuss, we stepped Earthside, making the twenty-five million miles from Venus-orbit to Terra Firma, in an infinitesimal fraction of a second. When I'd laid me down to sleep, it had been a ten-day excursion, even at fusion-powered constant boost. But you get used to miracles: I recognized this gimmick as an extension of the Broach-technology that had blasted me from the U.S.A. to the—

"Watch it, Winnie! It's a big first step!" I staggered, walking into twenty times the gravity I'd awakened under. Lucy grabbed my arm at the elbow, Ooloorie's extensors matching her action on my other side.

"You're telling me! You can let go now, ladies. I'll try walking on my own." I felt like an idiot. Thanks to my Earth-tailored genes, plus a little help from the "proper magnetic ambience," I soon regained my balance, but it had been a *long* time.

Ooloorie must have been away a while, herself: the lab we'd materialized into was disheveled, everything coated with dust—the parts that weren't covered with soot and itsy-bitsy pieces of paratronic components. Past grimy benches and dented equipment lockers, I could see we weren't in San Francisco—Laporte's smack in the middle of the continent, and the Rockies looked the same as ever.

During the century and a quarter I'd lived in the Belt, the city itself had metamorphosed into unrecognizability. We stood, sabotaged paraphernalia and all, in what appeared to be a forest clearing, not a building in sight, not even wrapped around the "room" we occupied. "Outside," beyond what would have been the boundaries of the physical plant, pedestrians were visible between trees: humans, gorillas, chimps, orangs, porpoises, and killer whales in wheeled frames. Strange beings who resembled ten-foot bundles of asparagus— not to mention the giant hairy crabs—were a bit unsettling. One of the latter waved at Lucy. She waved back. In the background, the mournful, mellow sound of a cello wafted in and out of the conversation.

Ooloorie watched my puzzled expression as I stared out over the wreckage. "Yes, they come from other planets we have discovered. The tall ones are called *Gunjj*, the arthropoids are *lamviin*. There are also *three* Belts in the System now, the Natural Asteroids, your Venus Belt, and now Neptune. Four, if you count the Cometary Halo. Over a hundred million 'planets,' ranging in size from a few hundred yards to—"

I listened to the invisible, unaccompanied cello a moment. Unbidden, words began forming themselves in my head, not by any miracle of technology: *"There are places I'll remember, all my life, though some have changed..."* Lennon and McCartney. Kind of appropriate. Muzak had improved. "What, no ring around Uranus?"

"Excuse me?" It was the dolphin's turn to wrinkle her features in confusion. Mine were permanently creased that way.

"Just paraphrasing an old commercial. Weird how the pronunciation changed when it started getting mentioned on TV." I waved a hand toward the jungle where a city used to be. "You were explaining..."

"It is still here, landling, underground, out of sight. If we had time, I could find your old house on Genet Place. There are still roads for people who like to drive, paths for people who prefer walking, but the Broach—"

"Does the real work of every former mode of transportation?"

Pride was in her voice. "Nine-tenths of the sapient population live someplace other than Earth. By earlier standards, every city on the planet is a ghost town."

Lucy snorted. "Gravity sucks! Nobody puts up with it if they—"

"Then what are we doing down here in Deejay's old workshop, when we could be up—"

The physicist interrupted. "But landling, this is not—" She indicated the corner of the area worst-destroyed. Nothing remained of the original time-machine. In its place—I'd never been able to communicate precautions about physical evidence to these people—a gleaming structure rose out of the ashes, reminding me of the early Broach devices, only about four times as complicated. Ooloorie had spent a busy week.

The cello-playing stopped. Across the blast-damaged clearing, the heat-scorched side of one of the larger trees swung open. "I trust I'm not too late," a high-pitched male voice sobbed. "Has anyone given a thought to tea?"

A bald figure with thick-lensed glasses, bow and cello clasped to his bosom, stepped into the clearing, tears streaming down his pudgy cheeks. He wiped his eyes, swallowed, inclined his head. "Please to be welcome in my home." He lifted the cello, nodded toward the blackened tree. "I, er... zis *unheimlich* looks, I realize. You zee, my mutter... zat is, I—" He stammered to a blushing halt.

"His parents wanted him to be a physicist," Ooloorie explained. "He had to practice the cello on the sly, hiding in a bedroom closet. Now I am afraid that's the only place he *can* play." She nodded in my direction. "Hirnschlag von Ochskahrt, this is Edward William Bear, the famous detective I told you about."

"Yes, but this feminine rustic hillbilly person, I do not—" He blinked, then noticed that the end-spike of the instrument was resting on his instep and gave a little yelp. Then he dropped his bow, stooped to pick it up, and whacked his naked scalp on the peg-head of the cello.

"Hillybilly?" Lucy exclaimed. "Say, buster, don'tcha know a San Antonio Rose when y'see one?"

Lucy sniffed with disdain at the laboratory beaker Ochskahrt had provided, just as she had glared at the plastic chair she'd been offered, before dusting it off with her ratty feather boa. The professor wasn't discriminating against San Antonio roses. I had been provided with my own unsanitary tea-receptacle.

Hirnschlag von Ochskahrt just wasn't very long on hospitality—or tableware. It was raining in the forest, now, and I had my first real taste of what Ooloorie had warned me about. Water dripped from the surrounding trees, gathered in puddles all around our feet—yet somehow never managed to get anything wet.

Milieu of contemporaneity, hunh?

"A voman," Ochskahrt squeaked, rubbing manacle-scarred wrists. "Much about her, I cannot tell you. Such zings as a rule, I do not notice. She frightened me, but I am afraid everybody does. Und such a great deal of money she offered..."

I rummaged through the debris for a household 'Com pad, found one in a wastebasket, a scientific Gigacom model, opaque white plastic, the height and width of a clipboard, but three-quarters of an inch thick—decades out of date even before I'd packed it in at Gary's. You pushed a button on the edge to summon up an onscreen keypad. I had some difficulty getting a file opened, charging it to my long-dormant home account. I began taking notes. "She give you any name?"

He shook his cantaloupe head, "Money only."

"I see. How about an address or 'Com number?"

"Tucker Circle, nummer nine und eighty. A big, dark old-fazhioned house mit real walls, glass windows, boarded up—"

"Hamilton House," Lucy interrupted in disgust. "That woulda told us, even if we hadn't had the medallion."

She was right. We'd both been there with Ed a couple of times in the old days. Never on a social occasion.

Suppressing a postmonitory shiver, I keyed the 'Com pad, entered the address, along with a query to the system.

"Well, I'll be registered an' licensed!" said a tiny voice. I looked at the screen in my lap. A cartoon gorilla stared back, blinking. *"First time I been up in . . ."* He paused for thought. *". . . in nine point five times ten to the eighteenth nanoseconds. 'Bout thirty years t'you, nake. Are you* really *on manual, old timer? Maybe it's a nostalgia-kick that'll catch on. Good t'be back in harness."*

Old-timer!

"Cut the comedy and give me information. What do you mean 'on manual'?"

"I mean, venerable friend, that everybody else uses the system more or less the way I do—or did." He gave a sigh. *"As* part *of it, using their brain implants. I—"*

"Implants?" I stopped, looked around at Lucy, Ochskahrt, Ooloorie. I'd wondered how she'd opened that door back in the Belt without— "You mean everybody—" They looked back, trying not to bring up the subject of future-shock for the second time in half an hour. I inhaled and accepted it. Lucy was right: I'm immune.

"Never mind that," I interrupted myself. "Tell me who owns the property at 89 Tucker Circle these days."

"You do—if you want it. It's abandoned property, up for grabs, like half the stuff within ten kilomiles of here. How about it? I can patch in a reputable registration company—"

I toyed with the idea. It would be kind of ironic if I . . . "Forget it. Who was the last owner-of-record?"

The gorilla blinked again. *"That would be 'way back in 219* A.L. *The name is 'Greater Laporte Hamiltonian Society (Norrit Gregamer Memorial Chapter)'."*

"But Norrit Gregamer died in 217 A.L.," I objected. And a good thing, too. He'd crawled out from under *that* generation's rock and begun trying to Hamiltonianize the Confederacy, getting his head blown off as a consequence. Some days, Murphy's Law or not, everything nice that can happen, does.

The cartoon ape glared at me. *"I said 'Memorial,' didn't I?"*

"No need to get testy. Maybe it's silly to ask, where Hamiltonians are concerned, but is there any individual owner connected with—"

"Sure, old timer—now don't you get testy, either, you don't look a day over ninety. The President, Vice President, Secretary, and Treasurer of the G.L.H.S. (N.G.M.C.) is listed as an Edna Janof."

"Great," I said to no one in particular. "She died in 217, as well." And I ought to know.

"I killed her myself."

6

The Whiskey Boys

JULY 16, 1794

"Ouch! Son-of-a—Hirnschlag, why are you sitting there?"

Clothed in phony buckskins, Edward William Bear stumbled into the false dawn of an eighteenth-century morning through the azure circle of the Broach, laden with copper-bottomed pots and pans, powder horns, a pair of flintlocks, and more knives than you could shake a stone at. They scattered as he hopped to regain his balance. Behind him, the circle narrowed, shrank, disappeared with a *pop*!

Ochskahrt rubbed a bruised spot on his backside, mumbling Teutonic apologies. Having given the terrified nod to fifty-year-old holos of Edna Janof back in the lab, now he was along—against everybody's better judgment—to identify the culprit in person.

"Sorry I'm late, folks. Ooloorie tried everything—

45

if she can't recover those settings, no one can." Ed recollected his awkward burden, laying it out on the ground beside me. From the casual nod he tossed me, no one would have deduced that we hadn't seen each other for half a century. "We had a devil of a time with Hirnschlag's fabricator—it was programmed to produce nothing but cello strings."

Across the clearing, a leather-clad Ochskahrt blushed, as if Ed had told the world of his secret collection of women's high-heeled footwear. No one had been able to talk him out of bringing the cello. "Please, my apologies to accept," the physicist said. "Zat my client the dewice vould sabotage, so as ze temporal coordinates to destroy after transposition, I did not anticipate."

I said, "It's okay, Hirnschlag, nobody could. She covered her tracks, our Edna. Hope we've come back in time to get here first."

"Me, too, Winnie," Lucy agreed, Ed nodding along to keep her company.

Water dripped off leaves overhead, accumulating in my half-tanned leather collar, running down the back of my neck. It felt appropriate. A good man was going to die today—all we were allowed to do was watch— and there wasn't a bloody thing we could do about it. I took the muzzle-loader my cosmic twin had handed me, a sour expression forming of its own accord across my face. Not wanting to need my Model 58 was one thing. The desire that I'd never have to depend on this chunk of outdated plumbing amounted to a religious experience.

In this decade of the 1700s, the lower left-hand

corner of Pennsylvania—where Pittsburgh boomed, a metropolis of a thousand—was reputed to be one of the most beautiful places in the world. Writers of the day, real estate salesmen I suspect, compared it to the Vale of Cashmere, the Scripture Eden, the Paradise of a hashish-smoker's dreams. I'd rather have been in Philadelphia. It had been raining here, too. Almost hidden by overhanging trees, a rutted trace wound through the hills. Now and then, it emerged into an open area ringed with blackened stumps or girdled and dying trees—hell, if the alternative's half a day's axe-work, why *not* let the damned things cut themselves down? The resulting rude cabin of un-squared logs constituted the quaint home of the eighteenth-century pioneer—accompanied, if said pioneer was well-off, by a quaint little annex out in the back.

Far below, muddy Chartiers Creek—according to Kropotkin Tours—coiled among guardian hills, clad in a mantle of many-shaded green. If it'd been the Monongahela, a flatboat, with a farm wagon perched on the roof, would have been winding its way downstream to what locals were calling Kaintuck, laden with squalling domestic animals and noisy, tousle-headed children. Or was that noisy tousle-headed domestic animals?

"Woulda carried other cargo, too," she told me. "A hundred thousand gallons of firewater're gonna go gurglin' down to the Spanish Territories this year, Winnie. Twenty-five percent of the stills in America were—*are*—in western Pennsylvania, pret'near half that number in Washington County, the very place we're standin'!"

Surreality hit me all over again. Even given a U.S. education, which ignores the Whiskey Rebellion, plus the fact I'd been playing with Ooloorie's universe-hopping toys the better part of a century, it was still scary to be sitting in this drippy woodlot, waiting to meet *the* John Holcroft.

Better known as Tom the Tinker.

Talk about legendary figures: How many movies, TV shows, comic books, and bubble-gum cards had been dedicated in *my* home-universe to the great-grandaddy of all tax-resistors, Robert Earl of Lockesly, aka Robin Hood? Or Lady Godiva *and* her chocolates? Throw in Walt Disney's "Scarecrow" adventures, you'll have a notion of the timeless popularity of Whiskey Rebel stories on the 'Com. Here I was, in the middle of a goddamned historic picture postcard, waiting for a guy who didn't even know he was the hero of it yet.

Also, I was trying—unsuccessfully, so far—to get a linen-patched lead ball started into the unrifled bore of the muzzle-loading pistol Ed had handed me. It was sticking halfway out, like an uncivil tongue. Disgusted, I flopped the semiloaded pistol across one knee. "Forget this time-travel crap," I muttered, massaging the inside of a thigh where the drizzle-stiffened buckskins Ooloorie had provided were sanding their way through my epidermis. I didn't seem to fit in either of the centuries I'd visited since waking up. "I'm going back into stasis!"

"Show him how to adjust his skinsuit, willya, Eddie? Lemme see that blunderbuss!"

Ed knelt, peeled back the arm of my Davy Crockett outfit, did things to the tiny panel painted on my forearm. The drip-dampness down my back was gone. I began feeling relief where buckskin had been chafing—an end to frontier diaper rash! No buckskins for Miz Lucy. She was charming in her pioneer sunbonnet and a hundred yards of pleated calico. Hems were worn long this century, necklines up around the ears. A stunning pair of Hessian Surplus galoshes completed her ensemble. It beat hell out of the mesh stockings and Merry Widow. Her designs, as well as mine and everybody else's—including a fringed leather cello-case—were the hasty result of an earlier bout with Ochskahrt's cranky matter fabricator.

They showed it, too.

She shoved back a sleeve, seized the pistol, tugged at a corner of the patch until the ball popped out. The charge I'd measured she poured into her hand, flipped hammer back and frizzen forward, dumped the powder on the priming pan. The pistol went off with a nonlethal *Whoosh!* Recharging the bore, she stretched a new patch across the muzzle, pressed the same slug into its center. With a sharp slap of her palm, the ball went flush, taking most of the patch with it.

Ed leaned toward her, slid eleven inches of razor-edged steel from the scabbard on his hip. Taking the blade, beveled on one side just for this task, Lucy sawed linen where it stuck out around the projectile. The hardwood ramrod slipped out of its little tunnel underneath the barrel. Lucy ran the ball home, seating it on fresh powder. She dusted the pan, closed the frizzen, lowered the hammer, handed the contraption back to me.

"There y'go, Winnie. Save that for yourself, case the Indians try t'rape you!"

"I *am* an Indian, remember?" It was the truth: Ed and I were full-blooded Utes, but it seldom came up in conversation. I indicated the pistol. "This operation's pointless anyway. I'm not going to shoot anybody, not at the risk of erasing the future."

Ed, still squatting, adjusted what looked like a barrel-wedge on the rifle he carried—I knew damn well he hadn't yet had time to load it—aiming at a squirrel two yards away, who'd been silly enough to venture out in the rain. He pulled the trigger. Nothing happened—

—except that the squirrel fell off its limb, onto its back in a pile of leaves. I counted seconds under my breath. After about twenty, the squirrel got up again, shook its head, chittered at us, and scampered back up the tree.

Ed laughed. "That's the point, O Chief of the Flatfeet: If we infiltrate the Rebellion, we'll be expected to help with the fighting. You can't go making somebody fall down and *not* have the sound and fury supposed to go with it. That would change the past, too— by our being burned at the stake!"

"They don't do that anymore." I turned to Lucy. "Do they?"

"A fine old custom, Winnie, still respected in some parts. But this here's Pennsylvania, not Massachusetts, an' that lead ball's designed t'disintegrate right at the muzzle. The Heller Effect'll be covered by blast an' smoke."

The Heller Effect: another leap that had occurred

while I'd been sawing logarithms. The same physics keeping me—and Clarissa's mitochondriasis—well preserved, were being applied to weapons these days. Admittedly, there wasn't much demand—being able to recover unscathed without so much as a headache to show for being shot, took a lot of the deterrent-power away from the concept of self-defense. Besides, Confederates believe the Tree of Liberty benefits from a little judicious pruning now and again.

For that matter, so do I.

Here and now, however, these phony flintlocks Ed had whipped up were almost as risky as the real thing—in terms of altering history. Talk about a shot heard 'round the world! However, we were up against an unprincipled enemy who *wouldn't* be taking precautions. For all we knew, the Edna Janof would be toting an anachronistic fusion-powered Gatling gun. We had to have *something*.

Our "something" wasn't much. In addition to the pistol, two feet long and about the weight of a twelve-gauge riot pump, we had the .45-caliber vaulting-pole Ed had just tested, of the pattern called Kentucky, but manufactured in Penn's Woods by old world "Dutch" (for which read "*Deutsch*") craftspersons. That was all the firepower we could afford, both in terms of mission-success and to all appearances. A long-barreled Penn-sylvania rifle represented about the same investment a family car had in the twentieth century. It made us middle class. Adding the pistol made us well-to-do. One more article of charcoal-burning hardware would have gotten us into the Social Register.

Ed would carry the handgun, I the rifle. He was

unaccustomed, like most Confederates, to the *idea* of two-handed weapons, let alone their practical application. Lucy tried to make up for her eighteenth-century feminine gunlessness by smoking a corncob capable of nauseating every mosquito within a mile radius. She had a little silver-handled poignard tucked away, battered and tarnished as though some British officer had misplaced it during the Revolution. A lot of war-surplus was still lying around western Pennsylvania. Ed had followed the same corrosive course with the one-shooter he intended carrying, battlefield pickups being easier to explain than unaccounted-for wealth. Each of us carried a blade, Ed's, the daggerish "rifleman's knife" he'd found in the replica catalog used to drive the fabricator.

The modern Bowie (or "Rezin," after Jim's little brother, the inventor) I was most familiar with wouldn't be developed for another generation. Which is why I kept mine—recovered from Little Sister by my look-alike—out of sight. It would pass inspection in an age of homemade cutlery—until some experimenter noticed you could slice a wagon axle with its stellite blade and still have edge enough to shave by. It was properly balanced, heavy enough for throwing, but I never have seen any sense in tossing the other guy a weapon.

Hirnschlag von Ochskahrt carried a hatchet. With a dead-flat cutting edge. We all kept a close watch on the clumsy physicist. In a pinch, the thing would serve as a club. Any camp-chores requiring the real thing could be accomplished with my two-pound Rezin.

Before leaving, I'd changed into the *actual* height

of Confederate style: thin-film skinsuits. Ooloorie and Lucy had been wearing their own all along, without my noticing. Successor to the rubbery smartsuit, frosty on the roll, invisible on the job, they were, among other things, pretty close to bulletproof. I was hoping they were hatchetproof, as well.

The four of us rested, waiting on the northwestern slope of a half-circle of hills rising half a mile from the lower summit of Bower Hill, residence of John Neville, local chief collector of Alexander Hamilton's whiskey tax. Neville's was the "Fourth Survey": Allegheny, Washington, Fayette, Westmoreland, and Bedford counties. The Chartiers Valley, southwest of Pittsburgh, was where the first shot of genuine Rebellion was about to be fired. We'd made a point of being out of range.

The rain had let up. I rose, half-leaning behind a small tree, and peered downhill. Neville's Bower Hill "mansion" was of two-story frame, forty feet by twenty, built on the highest part of the heel of the footprint-shaped hill. The hill itself was a half mile long, its toe pointing northwest to an abrupt end high over Chartiers creek. A ravine each side of the instep ran to a shallow depression behind the heel. From Neville's veranda, one could obtain a splendid view of the valley three hundred feet below and of the rolling country beyond.

According to the *Encyclopedia of North America*, consulted before leaving the twenty-second century, 1790's census had enumerated eighteen slaves on the estate. Also several white servants. The place was said to be "papered in the best manner, neatly furnished" with carpets, looking-glasses, a Franklin stove, pictures and prints, an eight-day clock, imported china, glass, and silver. There's no easy way to convey the wealth this represented in eighteenth-century Pennsylvania. Neville was a rich man. Maybe he had *three* rifles. At four hundred fifty dollars a year (several times the income of a wealthy farmer), tax-collecting was nice work if you could get it—and stomach it afterward.

At the southwestern verge of the heel, between us and the big house, were the Negro cabins; further up the ravine, Neville's own distillery, duly and obediently registered. At right angles, the barns and stables helped form a V, protecting the mansion. A road from the east crossed the instep, continuing down the hill to Woodville, country home of John's son Presley—the local militia colonel—visible beyond the creek through a lane cut in the forest. The two households had a system of signals in case of trouble.

Which was on its way.

It had been a while coming. On June 22, U.S. Marshal David Lenox had left the national capital in Philadelphia with warrants issued by the Treasury Secretary the previous May against local entrepreneurs who hadn't registered *their* stills. Pure political skullduggery: one of the biggest gripes Pennsylvania farmers had was that trials under the new Excise Act were held in the capital. Given the economy and condition of the roads, it might as well have been the Moon.

In April, at Hamilton's recommendation, Congress had authorized local hearings. But the warrants he issued later were written under the *old* law—though they weren't to be served until July. What it boiled down to was that Hamilton could tell the rest of the country how lenient he was—getting that nasty law changed—and still use it against those resisting his authority.

On June 24, Lenox arrived in Pittsburgh, stopping by the home of Hugh Henry Brackenridge, prominent citizen and professional mouthpiece. Anybody but Hamilton would have considered the new tax more trouble than it was worth. His assistants reported it was being ignored all over the States. Hardly a cent had been collected. Already it had cost the government plenty, prestige-wise. Witnesses against noncompliers had been assaulted, even kidnapped, their own stills bullet-riddled (Holcroft—Tom the Tinker—had called it mending, thus acquiring his nickname) and their barns burned, despite pompous threats from President Washington and offers of multihundred-dollar rewards. The law had also sparked establishment of "democratic societies" that would later coalesce into the party— the Democratic-Republicans—that even in my own over-governed universe would put the Federalists out of power. One of the first had been in Washington County, at Mingo Creek, in February.

In March, Neville and family had been accosted while riding home from Pittsburgh, and the chief collector later pursued by a party of sixty angry tax-evaders. Appeals had been made to replace Neville's more corrupt and officious assistants. Local magistrates opposed the law. Local Federalists had begged the Army for protection. "Respectable" citizens sat tight, ostensibly backing the government—they wanted to sell whiskey to the Army—and abandoned the smaller fry who had no recourse except violence.

Democratic societies continued springing up, passing seditious resolutions, encouraging loose talk about George Washington and guillotines. An old revolutionary custom, the erection of "liberty poles," was revived as a not-so-subtle warning. In this powder-keg ambience, calm reasoning was called for, but they were dealing with a government, here. On July 15—yesterday to us time-travelers—Lenox and Neville had braced William Miller of Peter's Creek with one of Hamilton's documents. Miller had told them to fribble off.

Knowing which end of a shotgun was which, they complied. But in mid-fribble, a flock of neighbors, there to offer moral and ballistic support, fired on the pair, sending Lenox back to Pittsburgh with dampened breeches, and Neville, in similar condition, here to Bower Hill. They should have realized that anybody from the area, equipped with the customary long-barreled rifle, could have eighty-sixed either of the officials if they'd been serious.

Meanwhile, the local militia Brigade Inspector, Dr. Absalom Baird, fed up with sporadic violence, well aware of its source, and with a keen appreciation of what militias are all about, ordered the arrest of Hamilton's minions, sending a Captain Pearsol to Pittsburgh and Holcroft to Bower Hill. This was the earliest we figured Edna was likely to try goofing history up. Tom the Tinker was due to arrive at daybreak, five minutes from now, with joy in his heart, a song on his lips—and blood in his eye. We were here to deal with Edna.

I was sort of looking forward to it.

7

The Bower Hill
Massacre

"Humans," *came the warning,* "five minutes remain!"

The small voice, nanoelectronic, was Ooloorie's, injected through a micro-Broach the fishy physicist maintained in our locality. I could hear her from the region of my collarbone, even without the headpiece of my skinsuit in place. The thing was useful, more than comfortable, but it made you look like a pantyhose bandit unless you took the trouble of adjusting its surface to your own likeness. Or somebody else's.

Another voice, muffled: "See 'em all right, Ooloorie? Pretty smart-lookin' outfit for a buncha easterners! No sign of Edna, curse the luck." Bonnet off, hood pulled over her eyes to provide magnification, Lucy breathed on my shoulder as we lay in the still-wet grass above Bower Hill. If Edna was wearing a skinsuit herself, carrying an energy weapon or any par-

atronic instrument, she should stand out like the proverbial damaged digit. Despite my own suit, my bones
ached from dampness. Some noble redskin, lurking in
the bushes, catching my death of lumbago.

Lucy looked like a molting frog. "Right smart-
lookin," she repeated to herself, "Too bad they're jer-
kin' the wrong quahog."

I peered at her, just to see if she'd really said that.
"Lucy, I don't know much about history—"

She leered at me. "But y'know what y'like?"

"Grrr! Those people down there *are* westerners.
Lewis and Clarke won't be doing their thing for another
nine years. *Pittsburgh* is the wild frontier!"

She was right about one thing: their mission to Bower
Hill was a wild clam chase. When John "Tom the
Tinker" Holcroft had been chosen to boss the punitive
expedition, everybody thought the bureaucrat they
planned to arrest for aggravated tax-collection had
retreated to Bower Hill with his partner-in-crime, John
Neville. But the militia's Mingo Creek commander
wasn't stupid—another party had been sent to Coal
Hill, overlooking Pittsburgh, to intercept Lenox in case
he was missed by the main force.

Knowing what was going to happen in advance was
less advantage than I'd imagined. The entire period of
history—like every other—was a matter of amateur
goodguys trying to outfumble amateur badguys. Rubbing a sore shoulder, I grunted, more at my own murky
thoughts than in reply to Lucy. Discomfort made me
homesick, reminding me of Clarissa. Clarissa, laid out
on a long white table.

This wasn't the first time—nor the last—that heroics had been displayed at the wrong time, in the wrong place. A couple generations from now, Andy Jackson would honor himself at the Battle of New Orleans (in my world: the War of 1812 hadn't happened in Lucy and Ed's) two weeks after the ink was dry on the Paris peace treaty. All Jackson's victory would accomplish would be to provide lyrics for Homer and Jethro.

Or was it Johnny Horton? In the dawn-lit distance, hard-ridden horses thundered closer. Holcroft's men, gathering at the Mingo Creek Presbyterian Church, had been exhorted to meet "opposition with opposition." If fired upon, they were to destroy any obstacle preventing their success. Too stiff in the joints to bother with my own suit-instruments, I strained naked eyes to see through trees. It was said of this era that a squirrel could travel from the Atlantic to the Great Lakes without touching ground. For once, what was said was right. The morning haze didn't help matters.

Below us, sudden activity: slowed to a walk, horsemen sifted from the woods either side of the road. I'd never realized you could *smell* a body of cavalry approaching. Not unpleasant, just noticeable. They dismounted, traps jangling, a congregation of around forty, few of them with guns, Dispersing like the guerrillas they were, they surrounded the house. They'd left the meeting about midnight. Tempers would be short.

The big front door of the Neville mansion lay open, cooling the place off. I could sympathize: coming from the high, arid plains of eastern Colorado, I'd once before endured Pennsylvania in July—police business, twentieth-century Philadelphia. The previous day's rain had made today's heat more miserable. Awakened by the commotion, a nightshirted figure stood just inside, ominously indistinct in the slanting shadows.

"It's General Neville!" Lucy whispered. "He'd just got up as the militia arrived!" I had the feeling this was the first of a long series of color commentaries. At any moment, Lucy, Ed, even Ochskahrt—anyone who hadn't spent the last forty years beating Rip van Winkle's ante by a factor of two—could refer to the computer on his cortex, tell us what was going on. Worse, Ooloorie was listening in, keeping a watchful eye on the four of us, also recording everything in color stereo for posterity and profit. I had nothing against the latter, but prefer making my mistakes in private. Telecomic supervision—and the commentary it engendered—was not progress. I determined to do something before it got out of hand.

Meanwhile, I'd rather watch events unfold for myself.

"Hello the house!" shouted a big man, clad in soiled leather and wrinkled homespuns. After a long night's ride, he'd do swell as the "Before" model in a deodorant ad. I was grateful all over again for the distance between us and Bower Hill. The fellow's hair was gray-shot, his scalp thinly upholstered, but he had big shoulders, hard-muscled forearms. He was heeled, but kept his flintlock grounded, butt-down.

There was an indistinct hissing noise. "Hello to you, Captain Holcroft!" the half-hidden figure replied in a low whisper that forced me to turn to my suit-ears.

"You have ridden hard to commit trespass this early in the morning!"

His attention on the house, the militia leader leaned the business end of his weapon toward the man standing beside him. He shaded his eyes to peer into the doorway, took a step forward, addressing the nightshirt. "And a good morning to you, Marshal David Lenox."

As a detective, most of my life is spent with the feeling I've come in at the middle of the movie. Time travel didn't make the feeling any better—now it was a movie I'd already seen, and it made my head ache. Even I knew about the historic mistake, Holcroft's taking Neville's voice for the marshal's. Also the subsequent historic sarcasm: "We are friends from Washington Township." American hadn't been invented yet; everyone had an accent, Holcroft's a slight Scottish burr. "We come as an honor guard to escort you to safety. Will you step out to parlay, sir?"

General Neville wasn't buying any. "Stand off, Tom the Tinker, stand off, I say! I've my wife in the house with me, also my little granddaughter Harriet Craig, and a lady visitor besides! I'll not see them come to harm! Stand off or pay the penalty!"

With that, as Holcroft realized his mistake, Neville swung a hidden brown-barreled weapon into view. Amidst exclamations, there was a *plop!*, a spark-punctuated orange flash, a gray billow of charcoal smoke. The dull crackless musket-roar came to us a moment afterward. The man beside Holcroft folded, his leader's weapon clattering across his body. A crimson pool began accumulating around his inert form.

A noise behind me. I twisted my neck. Ochskahrt had a look of horror on his face. Tears streamed down his cheeks. He clapped both hands over his mouth, waddled off toward a bush, the clumsy, gentle little guy.

"Oliver Miller," Ed muttered, closing his eyes. "William Miller's father. The poor old man will be dead before noon, first casualty of—"

"Ed?" I interrupted.

He refocused. "What?"

"Shut up."

There was a muffled boom of returned fire, interspersed with the *crack!* of rifled weapons, the sound of glass breaking. Someone screamed inside the house. Someone else began to curse. When a breeze next blew the smoke away, Bower Hill was without windows. The rebel militia retreated under covering fire, dragging Miller's soon-to-be-lifeless body with them.

Still the door stood open. I shook my aching head, about to comment on this tactical lapse, when several men rushed toward it. Lucy, straining forward, cried, "He's got a swivel-gun in there!"

Sure enough, I could see the brassy glint of the small cannon. The rebels saw it too, diving for the dirt. The General held his fire, not relishing reloading the thing. Small arms firing went on, no small percentage of it coming from the house. I was about to revise my estimate of Neville's wealth, at least in terms of firepower, when I realized that someone—the women—was in there loading for him.

"We oughta be closer!" the little old lady complained.

"S'pose one of them Hamiltonians is down there, *changin'* things? We couldn't stop it from here!"

"Quiet!" I shouldn't have yelled at her, I know.

Similar strain underlay Ed's otherwise deliberate calm. "They're *all* Hamiltonians in that house, Lucy, the original flavor. Even if we knew when Edna's supposed to arrive, there's nothing happening down there she'd want to change. This is a defeat for our side."

"A temporary one," Lucy insisted.

"One we mustn't interfere with." Then to himself: "What Holcroft couldn't do with a tachyon cannon!"

"Don't fret, honey." Lucy changed sides. "We're here t'practice lookin' without touchin', for the moment. Edna won't be jumpin' the gun, either—after the first real change she produces, she'll be flyin' blind as everybody else."

True, no one knows all the consequences of his actions, time-traveler or not. Gunsmoke drifted toward us, reeking of brimstone. I surprised myself, feeling a version of Lucy and Ed's combat itch. It was hell lying here, doing nothing. It drug on this way for twenty minutes, *bang!*-reload-*bang!*-reload, Holcroft and Neville shouting commands, the wounded hollering their heads off, when the clear *moo!* of a hunting-horn sounded from the house.

The yard filled with dirty-edged clouds as barrels burst through the grease-papered windows of the slave quarters, the noise as they flashed like a giant, ripping sheet. To anyone left in the yard, it was like being inside a blender. I counted four casualties after the first volley. Nobody stuck around for a second. Men and horses scattered to the woods. Someone emptied his lungs of terror, or pain. Not Ochskahrt, he was too busy emptying his stomach. The rest of my companions looked pretty solemn, too. My headache surged to new intensity.

Return fire from the rebels dropped off as they began retreating in earnest. The rout would take them southwest four miles to an abandoned Indian-fighting establishment. In later years, the Nevilles would claim Bower Hill had been attacked by a hundred-man, sixty-rifle party. According to the General's account, he succeeded, unsupported, in wounding several attackers, so discouraging them that they withdrew.

Don't ask me: I counted fifteen rebel guns, brought more for show than serious intention. During the half-hour engagement, I saw six of them fired, gunsmiths being scarce in eighteenth-century Pennsylvania. Henry Ford was right, about some things, anyway.

Meanwhile, the first real battle of the Rebellion was over, amateur badguys 5, amateur goodguys 0. Time for semiprofessionals to move along, too. "Onward to Couch's Fort." I sighed, trying to operate against the pounding inside my skull. "They tell me the news gets better after this."

I moved to rise—at least those were the orders I gave my hands and feet. Somehow, the message failed to get through. Lying flat on my stomach, I was overtaken by dizziness, then an urge to imitate Ochskahrt my stomach didn't have the coordination to obey.

I was paralyzed.

8

The Last Hamiltonian

Blackness never quite overwhelmed me. Instead, I remembered Edna.

Cheyenne, Wyoming, 217 A.L.: we were lifting her injured victim over the doorsill. It wasn't easy. The passage was narrow. His head and feet were hanging off the ends of the tool cart. The little wheels flopped and skidded through the gravel, the whole ungainly assembly threatening to go belly-up any moment.

My first acquaintance with the lady had been a raid she'd staged on my house in Laporte while I was trying to protect a client—the guy we were carrying. She'd shot me, a couple of neighbors, had my client imprisoned for murder, and generally made a nuisance of herself. That as an encore to butchering two bound and helpless old men—with a pair of manicure scissors, beginning with their eyes.

Now, outside, studded with machine-gun blisters and small arms ports, a big black hovervan waited with its back hatches open. Naturally, it belonged to Griswold's. But compared to Edna Janof, even Griswold's didn't know the meaning of the word *brrrr*.

Suddenly, around the corner slashed a yellow ground-effect machine, canopy open, a wild-eyed Edna Janof at the tiller, hair streaming in the wind. One-handed, she levered her flechette gun onto the edge of the door, its garbage can muzzle pointing at—

BLOMMM! BLOMMM! BLOMMM! BLOMMM! BLOMMM!

Steel slivers sleeted around us. Everybody went for the ground and their hardware at the same time. The cart tipped over, spilling its passenger but providing him with a shield.

I grabbed for my .41.

I won't even try conveying what all that weaponry going off at once sounded like. Somebody in the van let loose, concentrating firepower on the stolen sports car as it worked its way around for a second pass. Edna never did know when to quit. An explosion ripped its plastic skirt from hood ornament to trunk, flipping the vehicle over as smoke and flames enveloped it. The thing smashed through the flimsy wall of an abandoned warehouse. There was a flash that lit up all the windows, a bellowing of tortured steel and superheated air. The walls puffed outward, splitting at the corners of the building, the released energy flattening everything within a hundred yards.

We never did find Edna's body . . .

* * *

. . . next time I felt like noticing anything, I'd climbed a big tree when I wasn't looking. Curious, I peered between the leafy branches, watching Ed, Lucy, Hirnschlag scurrying like ants trying to move the stiffened body of a caterpillar. Trouble was, the caterpillar was *me*.

Sort of interesting: Ed had my sleeve up, jabbing skinsuit buttons, while Lucy slapped at my face. From this angle, it looked like I'd gained weight—have to watch that. He labored in grim silence, she calling my name (her version of it) over and over. Ochskahrt gave up getting in the way, sat hugging his rawhide-cased cello.

I tried yelling down to let them know I just seemed to be taking a vacation from my corpus delicti, but Ed snapped a sharp command. Ochskahrt ran off. Things went misty at that point. I was surprised: When you're a free spirit, *you're* the one supposed to get transparent. It wasn't that way at all. Everything else, rocks, bushes, people, became more insubstantial. You could see right through them. Including my oaken perch, which made me nervous—if the damned thing dematerialized, I might fall and break my ectoplasm.

A ghostly Ochskahrt came back with reins in his hand. On the other end was a horse, Oliver Miller's. Well, he wouldn't be needing it. I felt a tug, as if I were being drawn by a magnet. If I'd been religious, it would have been a good sign. As it was, I floated off my branch, toward the overcast. Last I saw of my friends, they had my mortal remains flopped over the saddle, leading it and the horse beneath, in the same direction the rebels had gone.

Meanwhile, I continued rising through the mashed potatoes: a thousand feet, ten thousand... by the time I estimated my altitude at a hundred miles, the sky had gone velvet, my velocity somewhere in the thousands of miles per hour. All around the stars were at their fullest-colored, planets circling some, against distant clouds of black-lit dust, faraway spiral galaxies. Whatever else was happening, the special effects were terrific. The voice of Bullwinkle the Moose kept saying "billions and billions and billions..."

The stars drew into spindles, one behind me a rich red, another in front, a deep blue. Blackness congealed into a tunnel I seemed to rush down at increasing speed toward actinic brilliance that resolved into a human form, radiating glory. A bandy-legged guy with a short haircut, heavy eyebrows, a two-button suit.

"Meet Edward William Bear—" The figure intoned as I sailed by. I'd heard that voice, but couldn't place it. "—who, at the ripe age of a hundred eighty, figured he hadn't lived long enough, and planned to tamper with Time itself. But, as he's about to learn, he hasn't traveled back to the eighteenth century at all. Instead, he has entered the Twilight—"

Floating past, I never got to hear the rest.

I began slowing, found myself in a harsh-lit room, filled with mist, surrounded by the faces of Lucy, Ed, Ochskahrt—my wife, my daughters, even Mom and the father I'd never known. Clarissa, dressed in a floaty gown (white was never her best color), stepped forward. "Go back, Win," she pleaded. "I need you, darling. Your work is not yet complete."

She hadn't complained about *that* for a long time.

I extended a hand but couldn't reach her. "Honey, I'm dead. I don't know what you and Ed and Lucy are doing here, but I'm going fishing with my pop—ask Mom where she put that pair of socks I never found after her funeral. Hi, Mom!"

Mother folded her arms, shaking her head.

Clarissa begged, "But, Win—"

"All right, so I *shouldn't* wear lavender socks. But you can come fishing, too, if you want."

They all started frowning. "Okay, Winnie," Lucy growled. "If that's the way it's gonna be, don't say I didn't warn you!" The acceleration started again, in reverse, out of the light, toward the ominous red end of the tunnel.

"Warn me about what?" I squirmed around to see where I was going. Ahead, a ragged mountain range was lit by flames. Waiting, green cape flapping, arms wide open, a hideous leer on the face as I bulleted forward, was another figure I recognized.

It was Edna Janof's portrait in the center of a U.S. ten-dollar bill.

9
Free Man's Burden

THURSDAY, JULY 17, 1794

From the day he was born, he was trouble.

John Baldwin never bothered to carry a rifle. When he wanted somebody shot, he just shoved the bullet in with his hairy thumb. Right now, he was thinking about it . . .

"But do you not understand, friends," argued a husky voice just managing to stay out of the hysteria-range, "that upon our leave-taking, our kindly neighborhood Inspector of the Revenue dispatched a servant to Pittsburgh, requesting—"

Another voice broke in. "Demanding, you mean!"

"Have it your own way, sir," the first voice growled. "*Demanding* that Major Thomas Butler send a file of bluecoats for the purpose of defending Bower Hill against further complaint from General Neville's dissatisfied custom."

"Nonsense!" That from an authoritative skeptic, the kind that's always wrong. "Butler is a friend, for all he commands the garrison at Fort Fayette. I myself fought at his side against Cornplanter and his savages. He would never stoop to defense of the Neville Connection against his—"

Nearby, soft, mysterious music issued from an empty grain bin. Ochskahrt had been instructed to avoid any composition written after 1794, but I don't think the message got through. He was playing "Stardust."

None of the contending voices was Baldwin's. A plainspoken man of the soil, he knew enough to recognize confusion when he saw it. And stay the hell out of it. Somebody else spoke, one of the McFarlane brothers, James or Andrew. I hadn't learned which was which, yet. "Inspector Neville will also have quilled a missive directing General Gibson and Brigadier Wilkins of Pittsburgh to call out their militia in aid of suppressing ours."

That observation earned assenting mutters, even ironic laughter.

"They in turn," Ed volunteered, "will pass the buck to the sheriff, asking him to raise a posse."

Scary silence. It would have been nice if he hadn't chipped in. I'd worried about this moment. We were strangers here—in far more than the geographical sense. None of these people were trusting each other, right now, let alone foreigners. Then the older of the McFarlanes, James, I guess, laughed. "'Pass the buck'? A clever turn of phrase, friend Edward, I must remember it!" General laughter.

McFarlane, a major in the Revolution, had been

elected leader of the expedition the night before—after a deal of enthusiastic buck-passing, whether they had a name for it or not. Individuals better qualified appeared less willing to have their names associated with rebellion. He'd ridden from Pittsburgh with news about the sheriff having been alerted and that seventeen GIs had gone from the Fayette garrison to Bower Hill. One of the buck-passers had been the local sheriff, John Hamilton. No relation.

A toothless ancient, wearing a faded black many-buttoned coat, cranked himself to his feet, raising his hands above his wispy scalp in supplication. "Gentlemen, I abjure you in the bowels of—"

"Bowels?" Ed was getting into the swing, and it made me nervous. "Oliver Miller lies gut-shot, and you speak of bowels? Who might you be, old man?"

"Why, he's old John Clark, pastor of the Bethel Presbyterian Church, yonder," replied McFarlane. The rebel leader pointed across the clearing, giving the geriatric case a nod of encouragement. "Speak up, pastor. What would you have of us?"

The old man pointed a shaky finger at McFarlane. "I would dissuade you from the enterprise before further bloodshed."

"Pastor, it's difficult," said another man, who looked enough like the Major to be his brother—and in fact was, "to comprehend the position of your church, its having supported the Revolution to the extent that Tyrant George was wont to refer to it as 'the Presbyterian Rebellion.' Has the clergy lost its love of liberty where whiskey is involved?"

The preacher, no stranger to whiskey himself to

judge by the veins in his nose, opened his mouth, said nothing, and closed it. At the moment, in the glare of yet another kind of morning after, the Bower Hill mini-battalion, augmented by an astounding force of five or six hundred men—"an expedition of over three hundred guns," history books said—called up during the night, were just realizing that they had the makings of a revolution on their hands. John Holcroft and his party were certain to be prosecuted unless they were supported by the surrounding community sufficiently to force events in some other direction. There was considerable debate. Some called, like Pastor Clark, for meek submission, others for compromise. The hulking Baldwin sat quiet in the background, propped against a wall, stropping a huge, crude-forged fighting blade on his boot-sole.

It had stopped raining twenty-four hours earlier. Still this place dripped. I lay a yard away from Baldwin, at the rough stone footing of a palisade of rotting logs, my breathing not quite so painful now. The unexpected aftereffects of forty-four years in stasis had left me weak and helpless through the night.

And perhaps envious. Holcroft and his men could cherish the satisfaction of having been in a battle, although Tom the Tinker's pullback to Mingo Creek Church hadn't been a bit less ignominious than our own to Couch's Fort, a moldering defense against the Indians about four miles southeast of Neville's place. I seemed to be no more than a casualty of lying in wet grass too long.

Ed sat beside me, the other half of the "Bear twins," new volunteers in the struggle against taxatious tyranny, fighting mad and fresh from the wilderness "west of here." Somewhere around Cleveland, we left it vague. Back in Ochskahrt's lab, we'd discussed using the name "Baer," Pennsylvania being crowded with immigrated Germans. The likelihood of running into someone who could handle a language neither of us spoke canceled the idea. "Bear" is an English name, and in a pinch could hint at our Red Indian ancestry. Nobody we were dealing with—excepting Albert Gallatin—had ever bothered learning to tell a Ute from a French horn.

It helped that we'd been at the ruins of Couch's Fort, where we knew they'd turn up the next morning. Excise-related encounters of the tar-and-feather kind had been accumulating since 1791. We gave them a story about having heard of the exploits of Tom the Tinker even out in the hinterlands of Ohio. It also helped that we'd brought our own guns, that sort of plumbing being in short supply.

For several hours after Bower Hill, I couldn't move a muscle. The condition was progressive: when I'd regained consciousness, even speaking was too much. I swam in a red fog thick enough to keep me from feeling much. Now and again, the fog would thin. I'd perceive that Ed and Lucy and Ochskahrt were carrying me, or later that I was belly-down over a saddle. Four miles through rough, almost roadless country should have been uncomfortable that way, but it wasn't. I didn't wonder until later whether Oliver Miller's horse would be missed by its inheritors, and by then there was too much company around to ask about it.

We'd passed my illness off as a minor bullet wound acquired at Bower Hill during the moment of greatest

chaos. Lucy—presented to the rebels as our cantank-
erous mother—had adjusted my suit, underneath the
buckskins, to simulate a bruised crease in my side. It
even seeped pink-tinged plasma, extracted from body
fluids, into the linen bandage she'd wrapped over it.

The bullet wound had also solved the problem of
credentials. These people were neighbors, in many cases
related by blood or marriage, engaged in activities con-
ducive to the sale of a lot of rope to the government.
Individuals were trying to decide which side to take
and whom to trust. But where there were wounded,
no one from the otherwise tight-knit Washington County
communities asked who they were or where they came
from. Their injuries were proof of their sentiments.

That time came, as it does in any room full of people,
when nobody could think of anything further to say.
The strains of "You Light Up My Life" wafted from
the horse-feed department, across the compound.

Baldwin stood, lithe as a cougar despite his size,
the huge blade swinging close to one knee. "Will no
one say 'enough' to this palaver?" He panned his glare
for everybody to enjoy, declaring between gritted teeth:
"I be but an ignorant farmer, no fine speechmaker like
some here. But the law of conviction has taken place
in my one breast to guide me to do right. Neville must
be made to hear his name called in a public court, to
undergo the ridicule of a lawyer, to be an object of
contempt for the public to gaze upon—else be put out
of the way like a maddened dog—are we to live free
of his annoyances."

His arm became a blur. *Thump!* Twelve feet away,

his knife had buried half its blade in the wall. Decayed flakes drifted to the dirt floor. "There, boys, I've cast *my* vote!" He set his mouth and folded his arms in defiance. It was the last he spoke all morning.

Major McFarlane was in no such speechless frame of mind. "Er, upon reflection, I have become aware of the rashness of this venture." Then he looked straight at Baldwin, who was busy trying to wiggle his toad-sticker out of a log—another terrific reason never to throw a knife. "But we have gone too far now to retreat. The militia will march in force to Bower Hill and demand Neville's resignation as Inspector of the Revenue—" There were murmurs, growls, some laughter. "Hear me! Upon which resignation, the General will be received as a good citizen and restored to the confidence of the people!"

Boos and catcalls. Someone moved to replace McFarlane with Baldwin. The Major laughed, allowing that would suit him as well as any other course. Baldwin blushed and hid his face in his hands. Democracy raised its ugly head: voting proceeded, and seemed to go on and on for hours, for these people a recreation as much as anything.

I huddled in a blanket, nodding in and out of blessedly dreamless sleep. That last nightmare had filled my quota for the next century. Somewhere between naps, Baldwin's "plan" to ambush and assassinate Neville was voted down, McFarlane's milder proposal adopted. That's when they committed their second mistake: to handle arrangements for the march, they appointed— a committee.

I shivered, turned over, and, to the lilting melody of "Over at the Frankenstein Place," went back to sleep.

I think Lucy put him up to that one.

10

Liar's Flag

"How you feeling, boy?"

"Hunh?" I woke with a start, seizing Lucy by the arm. *"Shhh!* You're not supposed to be here when there's..." I trailed off because there *wasn't* anybody else around. I'd laid my hand over the old lady's mouth. The eyes above it glared dangerously. The eighteenth-century man's-world business was the dumbest thing I'd ever had to deal with. I'd have given anything to have Clarissa with me. "Uh, sorry, Lucy."

I released her, propped myself on my elbows, took a deep breath. She hunkered beside me, a mischievous twinkle replacing the glare. I rolled over, stretched my arms, then stood up and began stretching everything else in astonished pleasure. I felt fine. I felt *more* than fine. "What's going on?" I asked. "What did you do to me? I could whip my weight in revenuers with one hand shoved up my—"

Pulling an earlobe, she said, "We didn't do a thing,

79

Winnie, not a blamed thing." Footsteps forced me to bite off a reply. Ed, poking his head around a corner, followed it into the compound. Behind him, Ochskahrt tripped on the gate-sill, ended up facedown in the dirt. Adjusting the big flintlock in his belt, Ed scuffed a moccasin and looked me up and down.

"You're in the pink, Win, according to your instruments. We've sent word upstairs to Ooloorie, just in case. She'll find out more if she can. Meantime, the weather's good, how do you feel about a four-mile ride?"

I shook my head and grinned. "Back to Bower Hill?" He nodded. I rearranged the big knife in my waistband, bent without the usual grunt, and grabbed the rifle where it leaned against a wall. I opened my mouth to tell them what a piece of cake it would be—

"C'mon, boys, we're burnin' daylight, an' there's *federales* t'put outa our misery!"

"Er, Lucy . . ." Ed stepped forward to whisper there still must be company outside. "Only one soldier was killed at the second battle of Bower Hill, and everyone who—"

She wrinkled her already-wrinkled face. "Spoilsport!" Then she said to Ochskahrt and me, "Let's get our carcasses outa here, 'fore he ruins all the fun!" She stopped me in the doorway as the others exited. "Glad t'see you up an' around again, Winnie. Had us worried for a while, there."

"I had *me* worried, too!" I stepped out into the noonday sunlight, and a ragged cheer went up. I looked around behind me to see what the fuss was all about, then realized it was for me. Five hundred men were seeing to their horses and equipment. Some "company." I grinned and waved, then started looking for my own horse.

Funny thing: It wasn't until this moment I realized that these were *dead* people, cheering me because I'd damned near joined their number a couple hundred years before I'd even been *born*. I'm certain they all felt alive, as unsure of their personal destinies—to me, the stale news of history—as I felt about my own. I'd been acquainted with a traveler from the distant future once, that flying-saucer jock I'd reminisced with Ooloorie about. Had he counted *me* among the already-dead? I climbed on my purloined cayuse and did the human thing: tried not to think about it.

My companions had acquired transportation. The march from Couch's Fort to Bower Hill, a pleasurable excursion now that I had the use of myself again, was completed by five o'clock that afternoon. The horses were left with some of the wounded or unarmed. They'd tried including me in that detail, but I refused to surrender my rifle to anybody. There was something special we'd come to see, and it seemed every yard along the way had brought me closer to full health. The whole world was celebrating with me, the sun shining, the birds singing, the crickets cricketing. The militiamen decided on a formal occasion, drawing up around Neville's bullet-riddled manor with drums clattering, fifes squittering, feet stomping in the closest thing Washington County could offer to military pomp and parade.

McFarlane and his officers took places on an eminence near the house to direct the "siege," but had agreed to try peaceable methods first. The forty-three-year-old combat veteran had been third-string choice to boss operations. When Sheriff Hamilton, the regular militia colonel, had refused, command was offered to young Benjamin Parkinson of Mingo Creek. He'd passed on grounds of insufficient military experience. David Bradford and James Marshall of Washington Town had been urged to take part, but declined, Bradford on account of conflict of interest—*he* was the local state's attorney. This was nothing if not a *respectable* insurrection. The laurel (or hemlock) was passed to McFarlane.

The troops continued spreading out. We four hung back, crouching under a tree where we could see the side of the building. Ochskahrt had brought his cello, thonged to his saddle, and had to be discouraged from providing background music. Sure enough, just before the militia closed in, valorous General Neville sneaked out, unnoticed by the volunteers, and burrowed into a nearby thicket, where he could witness the ensuing conflict without risking his aristocratic hide.

"Hey!" Ed shouted behind me.

"Leggo that pistol, Eddie, there's somethin' I gotta do!" Lucy struggled for control of the weapon, eyes trained on the brush a hundred yards away where Neville was demonstrating his courage.

Half-kneeling, I swiveled on my toe. "Lucy, have you lost your mind? We're here to observe. You said so, yourself."

"Sometimes I say stupid things!" She broke with Ed, whirled to face me. "Nobody knows how that skunk spent his evenin' in the bushes. I'm gonna insure he don't enjoy none of the excitement. Now mind your elders—gimme that gun!"

I shrugged, handed her my rifle. Crazy, but this was the first time I'd seen her without a weapon in the hundred-odd years I'd known her. Besides, she's one of the few people I'd trust with the future existence of Clarissa—and the entire universe. Cranking back the hammer—the "cock," a little vise with a chunk of flint in its jaws—she whipped a kerchief from around her neck, cramming it behind the frizzen. Giving us a wicked look, she hefted the gun—as long as she was tall—and pulled the trigger. At the same moment, Ed knocked the rifle aside. The cock fell with a noiseless, ineffective thump. So did Hirnschlag von Ochskahrt.

"There!" Lucy slammed the rifle into my hands, glaring at my twin. "See watcha made me do? He'll be seein' stars for hours!"

"You mean," Ed observed, "you'd deprive Neville of the sight of his house being—"

"Hold your muzzle, Eddie! Don't spoil the surprise." She paused, thinking. "Shucks, you're right, darlin'—I pretty near ruint it, didn't I?"

"I'd say so." Her husband sulked. "Besides, we have a theory to investigate for Ooloorie, concerning the good general. How can we do that if he's unconscious?"

"So we do," admitted the old lady. "I'm sorry."

"I know, Lucy, but we're not discussing your character." Before she could snap back, he pointed at the house. "There goes David Hamilton!"

Not being part of the electronic generation—no implant—I had no idea what they'd been arguing about.

Shooting Neville, with or without a nonlethal weapon, seemed like a swell idea to me. Hamilton, Sheriff John's young cousin—also no relation to the Secretary of the Treasury—had volunteered to take a stab at negotiations. Trudging toward the house with a flag of truce, he was met by Major Abraham Kirkpatrick—everybody and his bloodhound seemed to wear a military title—a family friend of the Neville "Connection" who had ridden out to join the defense.

Hamilton—as many Hamiltons as military titles—demanded in a stage-voice that Neville quit the house and resign his commission as revenue inspector. Kirkpatrick informed him, equally as loud, that Neville was gone. He, Kirkpatrick, had been left "to capitulate for the property." Hamilton stomped back to confer with McFarlane, then returned to the house. We knew he'd demand that six citizens be admitted to search for Neville's credentials as a revenuer and that this demand would be refused.

It took longer than I'd thought. I got pins and needles crouching under that tree, trying to keep one eye on the proceedings, one eye on Neville lurking in the bushes like a flasher, and a third on the unconscious Ochskahrt. At last I gave up—just wasn't spiritual enough for three eyes—and concentrated on the house.

Hamilton retreated from the porch, followed in short order by two petticoated women and a flock of scared-looking kids. This announced that war had been declared. Hamilton escorted the noncombatants away from ground zero. One of the bandaged horse-minders walked them in the direction of—

"Winnie! Ed! One of them two women's wearin' a

skinsuit!" Lucy pointed toward the road to Woodville, Presley Neville's home, where the escort party was disappearing over a hill.

I nodded, strode forward after them—into a sleet of gunfire.

It hadn't started all at once. Tentative, random shots were fired by the besiegers. There was a gleeful shout. Blocked from pursuing Edna, I turned to see the estate's outhouses set on fire—an underhanded trick, but war is hell. Burnt powder and hot lead issued from the mansion in reply. Firing soon became general on both sides. This time the rebels were better equipped. Having learned a bitter lesson about cross fire from the slave quarters the previous day, the militia posted themselves wherever shelter offered around the skirts of the mansion, shielding themselves behind trees and crouching below the verge of the hill. Their officers stood toward the east, near the road that crossed the depression at the rear of the heel of Bower Hill.

The party hadn't been going on very long before gunfire from the house ceased. A white flag was waved from a window. I watched, helpless again and not liking it, as James McFarlane stepped from behind a tree and took a breath to order his men to cease firing.

Bang!

A cloud of smoke billowed from the bushes where Neville lay. McFarlane slapped both hands at his crotch, fell to the ground. When it happens for real, there isn't anything funny at all about it. Femoral artery. He expired immediately.

Filled with rage I didn't have time to be surprised at, I wheeled, thumbed the hammer of the long rifle, and dropped it as the sights crossed the brush from which the treacherous shot had come. This time there wasn't any kerchief in the way. The pan spouted flame, and the weapon bucked with recoil. Ed seized the gun, too late this time. None of us said anything. Ed gave me a complicated series of dirty looks. Lucy patted me on the back. Ochskahrt would have snored if his molecular motion hadn't been halted. When we reached the spot where Neville had lain, there was nothing but crushed foliage and a French lend-lease military musket. Recently discharged.

Gunfire thundered once again, echoing from the surrounding hills. The battle resumed in earnest. Individuals, wounded or terrified, screamed and cursed. I did a little screaming and cursing, myself. I watched militiamen set fire to the slave cabins from which Neville's workers were again shooting at the intruders. As torches were thrown toward the big house, there was a shout. Kirkpatrick had decided to come out with his borrowed soldiers and surrender.

Under the hostile gaze of the militia, the regulars from Fort Fayette—all but the one whose body had been left inside the house—were disarmed one by one, their weapons discharged and returned to them. This was a strange war. They would be allowed to go wherever they pleased. But there was a sudden struggle. Andrew McFarlane emerged from the knot of POWs, holding Kirkpatrick by the scruff of the neck. Kirkpatrick wore the bloodstained tunic of the regular soldier who had been killed. "He thought to escape in the soldiers' midst before he was recognized!" shouted the fallen rebel leader's brother. I remembered how Santa

Anna had tried the same trick after losing the Battle of San Jacinto, in my history-line. It hadn't worked then, either. "You'll not get off that easy. Where are the rest?" Andrew McFarlane growled.

"The rest of what?" demanded the disgruntled officer.

"We're told you had seventeen bluecoats here. Now, we count but eight!"

There was muttering. Men looked around the darkening yard, swinging their rifles. The detained Major blinked. "Why, six departed this morning, I am told, Andrew McFarlane, if it's any of your business, and one cut down in the house, murdered by your—"

The bereaved brother backhanded Kirkpatrick. "And the other two?"

"Gone," whimpered the Major. "Deserted, I think."

Major Butler would later report three soldiers wounded. Two, indeed, were missing and were never heard of again. One of the rebels, in addition to McFarlane, had been killed. Meanwhile in the gathering darkness, angry men broke up furniture inside the house and set the place on fire. Articles of value were appropriated—the argument being that it was only fair, and with the elder McFarlane dead, who the hell was in charge to stop it? Neville's horses were shot, which I felt bad about, and I don't even like horses. Liquor from the cellar was brought out and distributed. Even the grain and fences shared in the general destruction. Of the dozen or so buildings on the estate, only the smokehouse was saved. Neville's Negroes pleaded that it contained their only food.

Neville had escaped. In a letter to Tench Coxe, he

would later place the loss at three thousand pounds, a fortune for those times. He'd taken it out of poor farmers' pockets, or intended to, *sic semper tyrannis*. By the time news came that Presley Neville and Marshal David Lenox had been captured, I was almost through feeling sick at all.

Grimy and soot-stained, I rejoined my friends at the tree that by unspoken consent had become our base. I'd been for a long walk. Edna Janof was nowhere near Woodville or anyplace else in the state of Pennsylvania as far as I could tell. The smoke was thick, and it was dark, but before I got there, I knew from hearing "Do You Really Want To Hurt Me?" that Ochskahrt was up and around again.

Goodie.

11

Mingling at Mingo

WEDNESDAY, JULY 23, 1794

Drizzle had been sifting through the trees.

"Here lies the body of Captain James McFarlane," Reverend Clark had intoned. I've always hated funerals. His words still rang in my mind. "Of Washington County, Pennsylvania, who departed this life on the seventeenth of July, 1794, at the age of forty-three years ..."

Hundreds of grim buckskinned figures had congregated about the freshly dug grave, we four among them, huddling in a cold rain timed just right for the ceremony. Even while I thought about it now, the log walls of the church steamed as the building warmed with crowded bodies.

"He served during the war," Clark had continued, "with undaunted courage in defense of American independence, against the lawless and despotic encroach-

ments of Great Britain. He fell at last by the hands of
an unprincipled villain—" bitter muttering followed
this last. I noted a satisfied look from Benjamin Parkinson, who'd been trying to convince the clergy the
rebellion was a righteous struggle. "—in the support
of . . . er, what he supposed to be the rights of his country, much lamented by a numerous and respectable
circle of acquaintance." This hesitancy pleased Parkinson less. The minister had finished, gratified at
having negotiated a tightrope.

There was still granite powder in the deeply incised
letters, the earth fresh on the excavation itself, when
we met a few days later. The guys in charge of the
Rebellion were just plain crazy for meetings. You
couldn't blame them: frontier life was nothing if not
dull, democracy a brand new toy. By the time they
tired of playing with it—at least in my universe—they'd
be stuck and wouldn't know how to get rid of the
damned mess *"Vox populi, vox dei"* always creates.

At the Mingo Creek Presbyterian Church, almost a
week after Bower Creek, the first order of business
was an angry letter from John Neville's little boy,
Presley, offered to the secretary by its recipient, the
carrot-topped Parkinson, chairman of the Democratic
Society. Ed and I squeezed into the tiny building and
slumped in the back, out of sight in the shadows. Lucy
would be outside somewhere—this being men's territory, no dogs or women allowed—listening in via her
husband's suit. After a week camping in the rainy
woods, we were dirty, tired of playing around with
democracy or anything else. I kept having lascivious

thoughts about hot showers. Even my stasis-tube at Gary's seemed like a nice thing to go home to.

Of the thousands ultimately involved, not more than half a dozen rebels came from the good-sized German population of southwestern Pennsylvania. Scrunched beside us in the rustic church, Ochskahrt kept his mouth shut, pretending to be one of them. Accustomed to civilized comforts, he was as miserable in these surroundings as the rest of us put together and still hadn't forgiven Lucy for shooting him.

Presley's letter, brought by some townies, had been preceded by a July 19th notice in the *Pittsburgh Gazette*, disavowing various notes—the equivalent of stopping payment on a check—lost in the destruction of Bower Hill. It made the rebels hopping mad; they were being called vandals and thieves instead of frustrated citizens attempting a redress of grievances. Parkinson hadn't read the letter, but he advised the group that Presley was a decent sort who ought to be heard out.

Craig Ritchie read the letter. Neville and the marshal had bugged out to Philadelphia—despite promises to those who'd captured them to stick around. The younger Neville defended Major Kirkpatrick's "intrepid" resistance at Bower Hill (i.e., he hadn't surrendered until he thought of it), boasting that though the insurgents might burn his own Woodville as they had his father's place, he had enough property beyond the poor farmers' reach to get by. A sour look on his freckled face, Parkinson accepted the letter back from Ritchie, stuffed it into his waistband.

"You all know the truth of what has been done," Parkinson said to the crowd, an aromatic lot: you haven't lived until you've spent several hours in a small heated room full of dampened woolens and muddy leather. At least another two hundred were sardined outside around the front door and windows, listening. "We who did it wish to know whether it was right or wrong, and whether we are to be supported in the matter or left to ourselves."

With that, he threw himself into a straight-backed chair at the rough plank table near the pulpit-end of the room. He stretched out long legs in high-topped boots before him, folding his arms across his chest.

His friend, James Marshall, shook his head. "The question is not as to what has been done, Mr. Parkinson, but what is to be done in future."

Parkinson conceded with an ill-humored nod. There were murmurings of agreement throughout the room.

Small, dark, and of a nervous disposition, local state's attorney David Bradford rose from a pew facing the table and began to pace. The little man wasn't a dollar better off than any of his neighbors, but his flamboyant clothing was imported, clean, and pressed. I grinned to myself. He reminded me of somebody's pet Siamese fighting fish: frilly, colorful, being swirled along in perilous, muddy water but eager to face whatever the currents confronted him with.

"Speaking for no one but myself," he stated, "my conscience sustains what has been done. I applaud those patriots now being characterized as rioters, and demand that it be put to vote whether those here present likewise offer their approval and will pledge themselves to support those who destroyed the house of the Inspector." An invitation to employ the ceramics for their intended purpose or abandon them, it was met with dead silence.

Marshall made throat-clearing noises. "The honorable George Robinson, Pittsburgh's chief burgess, is among us, invited by David Hamilton. Also Colonel William Semple, Mr. Peter Audrain, Mr. Josiah Tannehill, and Mr. William H. Beaumont. Before applying ourselves to this measure, might we not request of their spokesman, Mr. Hugh Henry Brackenridge, that he enlighten us as to views in Pittsburgh and his own opinions of the matter?"

The chair thought that was a swell idea. In Pittsburgh, popular opinion favored the "malcontents." Everybody knew it, including the city-father types whose interests lay with the federal government. A faint derisive hissing filled the room as attorney Brackenridge levered his bulk to vertical. Forced into delivering himself of an opinion, he resembled a trapped animal. I didn't know him well enough to realize this was normal with a man in the habit of playing both sides of the game at once. He glanced right and left, the eyes of the audience both attracting and repulsing him, then waddled into the aisle, advancing toward the chair.

At the head of the room, the rebellion leaders scowled.

He began. "Colonel Edward Cook—rather, ought I to address you as 'Mr. Chairman.' Young Mr. Craig Ritchie likewise, 'Mr. Secretary.' Mr. James Marshall—" Bitter sarcasm was in the lawyer's voice "—my kindly interlocutor. Also prosecutor David Bradford, and the good John Canon, of Canonsburg. I know you all as staid, comparatively conservative citizens, friends of order and good government who surprise me and my fellow Pittsburghers with your presence here."

Ed's suppressed laughter exploded in a snort: "He surprises *himself*! He got the invitation Monday and was so scared of the Rebellion he tore it up and threw it in the bottom of a closet. But then he pieced it back together like a jigsaw and told Presley, who urged him to come and persuade these 'leading citizens' along as witness—" A rough-clad unshaven citizen in front of us turned and glared. Ed shut up.

"I'm reminded—" Brackenridge hesitated as if in thought. "—of the Irishman, who, confessing to his priest a horrid mass of iniquities, was asked whether he could remember no good act as a set-off to so much wickedness." There was a murmur, not quite angry. These people wanted answers, not anecdotes. I thought he was an idiot not to see it. "The Irishman hesitated, seeming to recollect: 'Stay,' said he. 'I once killed an exciseman!'" He waited for laughter. What he got was anechoic nothingness. He shook his head, as if trying to wake up from a bad dream.

"Would I could paint," he tried again, "a portrait of the haste with which John Neville's son-in-law, Major Isaac Craig, tore the paper down by which the new excise office in Pittsburgh was labeled—the one opened to replace the house of the Inspector, and which is now, in anticipation of your demands, shut up. It is as if the Major had heard that story of the Irishman."

More nothing. The wooden floor creaked beneath his bulk. "Very well, then—" It came out in a squeak. He started again, two octaves lower. "I would venture to enter more seriously on the question put by Mr. Parkinson, whether those concerned in the destruction of the house were right or wrong in doing so."

He got his reaction, a general mutter of "About time!"

Brackenridge raised a fatty hand. "My colleagues and I can give no vote, as Mr. Bradford here demands. We were not sent to vote on any proposition, but to deliver an account of what has taken place in the town, to satisfy you, and show it is unnecessary for any force to come from the country to put down that excise office." Three or four cheers arose, subdued and short-lived. "But, although we are not authorized to vote, we are at liberty, as any fellow-citizens identified with the welfare of the country, to give our advice—"

"Of which you are supplied," Ed shouted, "with an ample surplusage!" The guy in front of us turned and scowled again. Ochskahrt jumped as if he'd been stung.

Brackenridge ignored the interruption, gaveled down by Cook. "Recurring to the question, the acts described at Bower Hill might have been morally right—I say '*might*'—but they were legally wrong. In strict construction, they were high treason—in which offense there are no accessories, only principals. They are cause for the President—in fact, it has now become his duty— to call out the militia."

That sent a thrill through the audience. Brackenridge had their attention. He climbed on his surfboard, curled his hairy toes over the edge, and started maneuvering for the crest.

"Now it is true the President will reflect on the difficulty of getting the militia to march. Your neighbors from the midland counties and the upper parts of Maryland and Virginia, disinclined toward the excise themselves, will be reluctant to move against you. It will probably be necessary to bring them from New Jersey and the lower parts of the states. The Executive, for such reasons as were given in the Philadelphia riot of 1779, will be disposed to offer you—an *amnesty*."

He left it at that for a moment. I shook my head in rueful admiration. The rebellion had only begun. Where the hell had the idea of an amnesty come from? It was like pulling the rip cord before the plane had finished taking off.

"But in order to obtain this amnesty," the lawyer continued, "application to the Executive would come with better grace from those not involved. It is not in your interest to involve us—let us remain as we are, in order to act for you as mediating men with the government."

"I have this day," interrupted Parkinson, color in his face, "spoken in overhasty praise of Presley Neville, upon receipt of his letter. Now this—this self-serving *lawyer* attempts to transform our meeting from that of aggrieved neighbors insistent upon justice into one of huddled, frightened criminals. I..." He stopped, speechless with anger.

A quiet voice took everyone's attention. "My brother lies dead by the hand of such a villain," agreed Andrew McFarlane. He moved through the throng with a black scarf bound about his arm. Brackenridge whitened, took a step backward.

"I suggest," offered Bradford, "that to obtain their normal span of years, the Pittsburgh delegates apply the grace of their backsides as mediating men with their saddles—yours, Brackenridge, would make a handsome target for Tom the Tinker!"

Everybody laughed. Brackenridge colored; the delegates looked at him as if to say "Another fine mess you've gotten us into." For practical purposes, that ended the meeting. Brackenridge had pointed out to the rebels what they were letting themselves in for. The Pittsburghers wanted to follow Bradford's advice and go home. The lawyer was reluctant: somebody— rebels, federalists, townspeople or their self-appointed leaders—might take retreat as evidence he wasn't on everybody's side at once. The crowd broke into small knots to talk things over.

The Pittsburgh delegation sort of half sneaked out to a nearby farmstead they were using as a local base. Brackenridge later resneaked back to the church, too late to get in on any decisions: Another conference had been called, for Parkinson's Ferry—an enterprise of Benjamin's older brother—on August 14. Like I said, those guys were crazy about meetings. We shuffled out, overflowing in anticipation of yet another miserable night on inadequate (but boy, were they authentic!) bedrolls on the hard damp ground.

Ochskahrt started tugging on my leather sleeve. I ignored him and turned to Ed, who looked as happy as I felt. "Did you see that gink in front of us?"

He opened his mouth, wrinkled his face, and sneezed all over me.

"Great. Swell. Marvelous. Well, I did, anyway, and he looked damned familiar."

"Fabiliar? How in Lyzadder's dabe gould dey loog—

waid! You're righd! Tage away dhe beard, dhe goonsgin gab, ad what've you god?"

"Edna Janof!" Ochskahrt exploded in a shouted whisper.

Ed sniffed. "Boy, is Lucy going to be sore."

I said, "Why? She was bound to show up sooner or later."

He said, "Because we didn't think she'd be here, dressed up like a—" But I was gone before he finished, pushing back toward the church, swimming upstream in a torrent. I checked my rifle-priming: There was a way to end this nonsense—shooting *Edna* wouldn't alter history! As I reached the door, I slammed into David Bradford.

"Oof! Your pardon, Mr. Bear. Stop a moment will you? I've a notion to chew over with you and your brother." The banty-rooster prosecutor shouldn't have known me from Adam. Rising from my sickbed with a phony bullet wound must have made me a bigger hero than I thought. I glimpsed Edna, then lost her.

"But I—"

"Come, man, there's no hurry to climb back into that mob—you'd only have to listen to Brackenridge again. See, he's buttonholed that frontiersman with the peculiar beard. What I have to say should interest you more." Tingling with frustration, I struggled to get free, but he had a death grip on my own buttonholes. The crowd continued flowing out of the building like the dozen clowns that get out of their tiny car at the circus. Between buckskin-clad shoulders, I caught tantalizing glimpses of Edna conversing with Brackenridge.

The pressure forced us out into the churchyard. "All right, then, Bradford, what would you have of us?"

He glanced around—silly, we were surrounded with humanity—leaned toward me, stood on his toes, and whispered: "We want you to help us with the Pittsburgh–Philadelphia mail, day after tomorrow!"

"Help you?" Something vaguely historical nagged at the back of my mind. I didn't like the feel of it.

"Help us," replied the fiery prosecutor. "We're going to rob it!"

12

Assault on a Snail

JULY 26, 1794

A swell day for a robbery.

The morning of the twenty-fifth had arrived with the proverbial good news and bad news: We didn't have to hold up the U.S. mail after all on the day Bradford had suggested; we got to wait until the day after that.

Today.

To say I was apprehensive would have been to understate things. Just like saying that I was quaking in my rustic brown suede shoes. I didn't like this idea. As a many-times retreaded expoliceman, I was more comfortable being on the other side of the law—whenever it would let me. Never having been an Adam Ant fan (I'd always thought "stand and deliver" was the way ostriches laid eggs), I was learning this highwayman racket the hard way—on-the-rob-training.

I couldn't complain about the scenery. There was a

pleasant breeze. The sun was shining as if it had an extra quota of hydrogen to use up. The birds were singing their tiny lice-ridden heads off, high in the leafy branches above me. A tiny gray rabbit galumphed over to see what I was doing with that pretty roll of soft white paper. I shooed him away. A person needs *some* privacy.

The delay had been occasioned by three unforeseen factors. First, that evening at the rain-soaked campsite our Confederate delegation had staked out within fog-bound sight of the Mingo Church—altogether too convenient to the cemetery to suit me—I'd had another attack of the poststasis horribles. Nothing terminal, it felt like the flu.

Second, David Bradford, attorney-out-law, had experienced a severe attack of his own—professional conscience. It would scarcely be suitable for the state prosecutor to be seen bossing an armed robbery. Would it? He was trying to invent the term "conflict of interest." Anyway, he bowed out, abandoning the caper he'd himself proposed, while offering his cousin, William Bradford, as a surrogate. David Hamilton—I don't know what kind of attack he was suffering—sent his own cousin, a fellow he introduced as John Mitchell. Gertrude Stein and William Shakespeare to the contrary, maybe there *is* something in a name.

Rough-hewn reliable John Baldwin sent his nearest relative—himself. I took pleasure in the brief, happy fancy of sending "cousin" Ed in my place, but it developed he was entertaining similar ideas about me. Besides, we were both going to be busy that day—

robbing the mail with cousin Bradford, cousin Mitchell, and plain, unadorned John Baldwin.

Now, a dozen yards through a heavy screen of trees, I could hear our horses whickering, the low voices of my fellow conspirators. I stayed where I was, squatting under a sycamore, allowed myself a cigarette. The rabbit came back. I chased it away again. I don't know what I've got, but St. Francis can have all of my share he wants.

The third reason for delay was that, had we decided on the twenty-fifth of July, the Pittsburgh–Philadelphia mail wouldn't have been there to rob. Neither rain nor sleet nor dark of empty slogan could keep wheels set in motion by Ben Franklin from rolling, even through the wilds of Pennsylvania. Every other week. Someone—rather typical in amateur revolutions—had gotten the schedules mixed; we didn't receive word of our reprieve until the last minute.

I rose, disposed garments and weapons about my person, and limped back from my seventieth trip to the bushes that afternoon on the road to our assignation with history. It was just in time to interrupt an argument.

"Y'can't *do* this to me, Eddie!" Lucy was yelling at Ed, while Ochskahrt hid his face in embarrassment. The horses were munching their way through tender growth encouraged by the past days' rain. Our rebel allies were scouting up ahead. We weren't quite near enough Greensburg yet to intercept the mail, but it paid to be cautious.

"Lover's spat?" I asked with an amiable smile I didn't mean, balancing my rifle across the saddle while

I tried to figure why it was taking me so long to learn
to mount a horse. She pitched a shoe at me—Lucy,
not the horse. I was grateful it was her husband's moccasin, not one of her own Hessian Army surplus or a
cast-off iron number. Ed lay against a sun-warmed rock,
barefoot, with a straw thrust between his teeth.

"Strategy session," offered Huckleberry Bear, spit-
ting a bit of straw.

"We're just discussin' business at hand, Winnie."
She set her hands on her hips and stuck out her chin.
"See here, I always did wanna pull a genuine holdup.
I'll be dogged if I'll be left outa this one!"

"Lucy, do you mean—" I was still trying to get a
foot in the stirrup. "—that we've stumbled across
something you *haven't* done already?" Pausing with
the cavalry-practice, I grinned. "She must be getting
old, Hirnschlag. I never knew anyone who could stop
her from doing what she wanted—or her to stop and
argue about it." The second moccasin followed the
first, catching me on the nose. I ducked behind my
horse as her hand went to the skillet tied to her saddle,
used for fatback and navy beans cooked over the campfire.

My horse cooperated by whipping his head around
to bite me. Ed wasn't much use in this discussion. He
was rolling on the ground, laughing. "You think anyone
could stop her if she didn't want to stop herself?" he
wheezed. "Come on, Lucy, 'fess up so we don't have
to speak of you in the third person anymore."

The old lady glared at him, glared at me, and even
included Ochskahrt, who cringed behind the cello case.
"Consarn you both, you've got me. Now that Edna's

here, there's another job needs doin', an' I'm the one t'do it!"

Ed nodded. "Then it's settled. You take the west branch at the next fork; we'll head east to Greensburg. You're a better shot than anybody here, and just to show you I'm sincere, look what I brought you." He reached behind himself, stretched out a suede-wrapped package. Lucy untied the thongs, dark eyes lighting like a child's at birthday time.

"A brace of pepperpots! For *me*? Eddie, y'shouldn't have!" She was sentimental about the damnedest things. I thought she was going to burst into tears. Glistening on the butterscotch-tanned leather was a pair of strange-looking flintlocks, each with a complement of seven barrels, each marked "H. Nock, London" within the scrolls engraved on the lockplates. Not what you'd call high-tech firepower—you had to charge the flash-pan for each shot—but impressive nevertheless, for the just-post-Revolutionary period. She raised her skirt, looking for garters to tuck them into.

"Careful with those," her husband observed. "They're real—anachronisms that won't be invented for another five or six years. Ooloorie sent them through before we left this morning, at my request. We need the clout—history won't be changed by killing Edna Janof."

"You bet your sweet turtle it won't!" Lucy said, giving up on garters and tucking both weapons in her waistband. "But all that's standin' b'tween Albert Gallatin right now an' a case of Hamiltonian wet-work is—"

We were interrupted by horse-clatter. Baldwin rode

back into our midst, followed a minute later by Mitchell and Hamilton, riding together. Horses were another commodity that, like rifles, were scarcer in this century than the movies show.

Mitchell, unlike his twentieth-century namesake, was a small man, wiry and dark, with a nervous intensity that set everyone else on edge. He was one of those individuals whose shaving habits are hard to figure out: If he never shaved, why wasn't his beard longer? If he did, why was his face always covered with hair a quarter inch too long to call stubble? He smoked a cigar—I hadn't known they did that in 1794—much like his beard: If he never lit a new one, why did he invariably have a two-inch butt protruding from his face? If he did, why was it never longer than two inches?

Hamilton, on the other hand, looked like all his cousins, tall, fair, bulky. In place of the usual rifled Kentucky, he sported a double-tubed scattergun, about eight-gauge. Confronting him in anger would be a bit like staring into a pair of garbage cans. I approved.

We climbed aboard our all-terrain vehicles. The road ahead was clear. The scouting party had laid out a course that would avoid the town and any farmsteads in the area. "Something I'd like to ask about," I said to Baldwin, riding ahead of me. "If we're going to play highwaymen, what are we going to do about masks?"

Baldwin turned his treelike torso in the saddle, staggering his horse. "What do we want with masks, friend Edward?"

"That's 'friend William.' Edward's my brother over there. Masks are customary when essaying a holdup, or so I hear is the current fashion on the Continent."

"Grrrrr!" Mitchell offered. "We have a continent of our own, nor shall we be like Englishmen, hiding our faces in defense of liberty!" Hamilton nodded agreement.

I shrugged, misquoting: "Masks? We don' need no stinkin' masks!" Ed grinned but kept his mouth shut. I was about to mention the Boston Tea Party, where Indian disguises had been de rigueur, when we came to the fork Ed had mentioned.

Lucy reined to a stop. "Guess I'll leave you boys to your fun an' games. I got business over t'Mr. Gallatin's place."

"Yes, Mother," Ed replied, earning a poisonous glare. "Don't shoot anyone I wouldn't." This time I was the prudent one.

"You boys be good. Eat your galoshes an' wear your spinach. You find anything interesting in the mail, be sure an' let your Auntie Ooloorie know about it. She'll pass it on." We nodded and took our separate paths, Ochskahrt nudging his horse Gallatinward behind her, his rustic instrument case bouncing against his thigh.

Minutes later, to the lingering memory of "I came to Pennsylvania with a cello on my knee," we found a place for bushwhacking, where the path curved toward a ford in a creek, and arranged ourselves for the ambush. Then we waited. And waited. Another few centuries, and there were horse-sounds in the distance, their source concealed by heavy foliage. I didn't seem to be learning the Junior Woodchuck routine. When the post-rider appeared around the bend, I was surprised to see him leading a spare cayuse whose hoofbeats I hadn't been able to discern from those of the first. It made sense. An ancient Roman idea, the Pony Express with waiting relays of fresh mounts, hadn't been reinvented yet. I was even more surprised to see that the mailman wasn't armed.

Bradford and Mitchell had disposed themselves on either margin of the rutted road, this side of the bend. As rider and horses passed, they stepped into the trace behind him. Baldwin, hiding with Ed across the road from me, took this as his cue. He rose, strode into view, armed only with the knife he left in the scabbard at his waist. "Afternoon, postman. What new tidings might you be bringing to the world from Pittsburgh Town?"

The rider reined up, his trailer bumping its nose on the tail of his own mount. "None so diverting as to occasion a delay of the United States mail, Mr. Baldwin."

The big man started at being recognized by someone he didn't know. There was a metallic triple *clack* behind the rider as Mitchell and Bradford hammered back their weapons. Baldwin sighed. "Give your pouch to me, rider, and be on your way. Tell the authorities in Philadelphia it was Tom the Tinker's men relieved you of your burden."

The mailman sat and thought it over. He was a kid, maybe seventeen and blondly whiskered, clad in the same buckskins everybody else wore. Then his leather-fringed shoulders slumped. He turned in the saddle, reeled the spare mount in like a jigged codfish, and stretched to reach back for the pouch. And turned around again with metal glinting in his fist.

Craaack! A beam of emerald, bright and solid as if

made of steel, spiked toward Baldwin. There was a scarlet-misted explosion. The rugged woodsman's headless body sank to its knees, collapsing forward into the dust.

13

TABERNA EST IN OPPIDUM

Splat!

Ed fired his weapon. I felt the numbing tickle of the Heller-field brushing past my left elbow. A sulfurous billow of black-powder smoke spread across the road toward me. Bradford shouted, "In the name of God!" his horrified eyes glued, with Mitchell's, to the ruined form of Baldwin.

Boom!

Even so, it caught me by surprise. Bradford's double-barreled shotgun spoke as the rider turned toward his terror-filled voice. The charge took the delivery boy in the forearm, almost unseating him. He screamed with pain.

Things started happening faster, then. Where the open features of a rustic youth had occupied the front end of the rider's head, now a gruesome swirling was

109

displayed. Moans arose from our eighteenth-century companions. The rider shrieked again as a *pop* and *crackle* at his damaged wrist announced, with a curling wisp of smoke, the demise of a twenty-second-century skinsuit. Blinded, the rider peeled away his thermoplastic head-covering to reveal the hate-filled face of Edna Janof, girl Hamiltonian. Leaning over, she hissed at me, between clenched teeth. *"You Confederate son of a bitch!"*

"Look out, Win!" That was Ed, trying to get his pistol charged again.

The woman ignored him, looking straight at me, brought her laser to bear as I fought my cumbersome rifle into line. Before I could get the sights on her unprotected visage, Bradford's mighty weapon bellowed again, the shot-column missing Janof but disturbing her aim. The beam leaped out with a *craaack!* A tree behind me puffed into flame. Her horse reared, gave a leap, and was off down the trace, dragging the spare behind.

I snapped out of slow motion. Ed's gun went off. Mitchell's rifle banged. The second horse tumbled, skidding in a cloud of smoke and road dust, a mass of soul-rending screams, flailing leather, kicking legs. The men yelled at one another, ran around like stirred-up ants. Edna's back dwindled until my brass front sight covered her.

It was pointless trying. I eased up on the trigger. The wounded horse lashed its head back and forth as it lay bleeding into the ground. Unable to take it anymore, I "finished" the animal with fake gunfire and a liberal spray of stasis-juice.

Edna, of course, was long gone. A pause for breath-catching, blinking, and reloading.

"Good god, what a mess!" I rose, wiped my hands on the thighs of my buckskins. My dry cleaner would never speak to me again. Whoever it was—Gilbert Roland or Ed Sullivan—who observed that a police-man's lot is not a happy one didn't know the half of it. I'd never had to cut a horse's throat before.

"Here, Mitchell. Do you intend eating what you kill?" The poor guy turned green and looked away.

The buckshot-spatter from Bradford's scattergun, along the animal's side, was incidental, but Mitchell's .45-caliber linen-patched ball had hit dead-center in the unlucky stallion's second-most-sensitive spot. From there, it had plowed through the intestines and dia-phragm, entering the rib cage to collapse the right lung and shatter miscellaneous bones before making its gory exit. Just missing the heart.

"First-rate marksmanship," I observed to Ed—if that's where Mitchell had been aiming, and we didn't ask. "Just the way you'd want to take a running elk."

"A pox upon such marksmanship!" Bradford was sorer than a boil—an appropriate turn of phrase, con-sidering it meant that he and Mitchell had to continue riding double. "And what, pray tell me, is an elk?"

I cleared my throat, grinned at Ed. "A rather large, mulelike horned creature we have out in Cleveland?" my partner suggested.

"Yeah," I agreed. "We hunt them with large sticks, called Elk's Clubs." Ed glanced at my scarlet-edged Bowie, then at my midsection. Bradford and Mitchell looked at each other and shrugged. Being twin brothers made you crazy.

The highwayman business is overrated. It took all four of us, straining and cursing, to roll the euthanized animal's carcass over so we could get at the blood-soaked post-bag that had dug its way into the dirt, halfway through to the Indian Ocean. There was a bad moment when Ed's disintegrating pistol-ball failed to damage the brass lock. I was thinking less and less well of our measures in the armaments area, with the memory fresh of trying to stop a bloodthirsty, skinsuit-protected Hamiltonian with what amounted to a Captain Video paralysis ray. My "twin" made lame excuses about having cast the ball, for antipersonnel purposes and reasons of economy, from brittle pewter. I saved a remark about the way we do things in Cleveland. The others were so shaken that they went along with the gag.

I levered the bag open with the same Bowie I'd finished the horse with, trying not to slice the hardened alloy of the hasp too cleanly. Then, as the others began to recover and were congratulating themselves on a daring daylight robbery, I trudged back a disgusted hundred yards to clean my forearms and the knife in the creek. And to do some throwing up. No tiny furry rabbit came to see that. I kind of missed him.

"One, two, *three*!"
"Oh shit! Look out for that stirrup!"
Thump! Bradford staggered, having ducked the stirrup, only to get bonked by the dead man's boot-heel, right on the top of his cranium. At least he still had a

cranium to get bonked on. The horse shied, and the headless body flopped into the dirt. I collided with Ed as we chased after the animal. Then it was John Mitchell's turn to make a dash for the creek with his hands over his mouth. Bradford's turn had come right after mine. Tender stomachs, these colonials.

Slinging the remains of poor courageous Baldwin over the saddle of his horse had proved to be as ugly a task as finishing off the spare and rolling it over to retrieve the mail. Hell, I'd gotten to like the man. His horse kept objecting, and, when Mitchell returned, I heard him mutter something to Bradford about Baldwin's demise being the work of the devil. I suppose it might seem that way to someone who'd never seen a laser. If Edna had intended altering Confederate history, she was succeeding. At this rate, we'd be back in the Dark Ages any moment.

Of the mail, we left everything behind with the horse that had carried it—dead letters in more than one manner of speaking—except those all-important packets from Washington and Pittsburgh we'd been sent after. There followed a brief, subdued ride to Canonsburg, during which Ed caught Lucy and Ochskahrt up on current events. I wouldn't get to hear the gossip myself until later, being unwilling to risk showing my suit, after the run-in with Edna. It didn't occur to me until that moment that I might have talked to them while washing at the creek. I'd been preoccupied.

As arranged beforehand, Benjamin Parkinson met us on the Canonsburg road. His task—these having been parceled out in a manner consistent with the custom requiring every member of a lynch-mob to place his hand on the rope—was to deliver our ill-gained loot to prosecutor David Bradford. Receiving stolen goods didn't disturb his fine sense of professional ethics. Him we rendezvoused with in the parking lot of Canonsburg's only tavern.

"You've done a fine, brave job, lads," the lawyer offered. "History will vindicate the bloody work you've dedicated yourselves to this day. For now, you'll have to be satisfied with Mr. Westbay's cellar and the products of his still." John and William nodded, allowing as how an Imperial gallon or two might be adequate recompense for what they'd been through—for starters—Ed and I half a beat behind them. There were an even six of us now, involved in the secret conspiracy: me, Ed, Mitchell, Bradford's cousin, Parkinson, and the state's attorney. The concepts of leakprooficity and "need to know" were yet to be invented, never would take root in the Confederacy the way they had in my time-line.

The "town" of Canonsburg consisted of a half dozen ramshackle buildings clustered around the local nightspot Bradford had met us in front of. We were shortly joined by James Marshall, whom we'd met at Mingo Creek, dour Alexander Fulton, and a Mr. Lochry we were introduced to. The individualists of the Rebellion were on comfortable ground again, having acquired the beginnings of yet another committee. Together, the nine of us (nine!) headed for the front door of the Black Horse Tavern (Henry Westbay, Prop.—and he made it ten) to open the Philadelphia mail as an official act of war, in the august presence of local patriarch John Canon (eleven) and his comagnate, Thomas Speer (twelve—and if one more clown showed up, I was going to quit). The Prop. met us at the door.

Rather than inviting us into the dark, smoky tavern, beginning to fill up at this hour of the afternoon and smelling of last night's beer and bear-grease, Westbay, the fattest man I've ever seen, motioned to us. We followed him out back to a grape-arbor, where the sun dappled its way through the leaves onto a stained, unpainted table. A plain girl, already promising to follow in her father's fatsteps, brought us refreshments in unsanitary mugs on a matching unwashed tray.

Ed twisted the wounded padlock off the mail pouch. Inside the well-used leather sack was a bundle of epistles. Lochry, a rough-voiced man with the air of a retired sea-captain, grabbed the bag by its corners and upended it on the planking. A couple dozen documents spilled out. David Bradford pulled a wicked-looking folding knife from his boot, levered it open, began breaking seals. The contents were interesting. I wasn't sure what use they were as counterintelligence.

That great little letter-writer, Presley Neville, had written, griping in a bold, rounded cursive, to his father-in-law, General Daniel Morgan, about the uppity ungrateful attitude of nontaxpaying peasants. Another general, John Gibson, expressed similar sentiments to Governor Thomas Mifflin. Prothonotary James Brison (whatever the flaming hell a prothonotary was) also attempted to bend the Governor's ear long distance, on the volatile subject of liquid assets and the so far non-existent revenue therefrom. Fort Fayette's Major Thomas Butler did his complaining to Secretary of War Henry Knox.

Last, but parsecs away from least, was an unsigned letter Bradford opined might be in the handscrawling of somebody called Edward Day, addressed to Alexander Hamilton. Himself. I was amazed what terror mention of that name could inspire. For the first time, unspoken doubts about the wisdom and morality of this afternoon's activities circulated among the conspirators. I shivered myself, remembering my out-of-body fever-dream and how it had ended. Day, if that's who it was, advised Hamilton to send troops in whatever number could be mustered, reinforcements to follow. He cautioned that even twenty-four hours' delay could prove disastrous to the continued existence of the Republic, and that local measures would be taken to secure things at this end, through the arrest, fair trial, and prompt execution of the ringleaders.

Not necessarily in that order.

I glanced at Ed, wishing to hell I'd endured an implant operation, or had taken the chance this afternoon to speak to him alone. Albert Gallatin, who as far as I knew hadn't stirred a finger yet, was at the top of the list. Even Lucy might have trouble fending off the attack this letter promised. And the handwriting looked like Edna Janof's to me.

David Hamilton, of course, pressed for an immediate uprising. I wondered who he'd get to substitute for him when that came to a head. Maybe I was being unfair, but watching a good man die can be hard on you. So can cutting a horse's throat. Or seeing your heroes up close.

Hamilton (David, not Alexander) might have known better, though. We rugged individualists had our ways of doing things. Yet *another* militia-meeting was decided on, for the afternoon of July 30, just outside of Pittsburgh, at a place called Braddock's Field—the twentieth-century site of a similarly named Pittsburgh suburb and current property of somebody named George Wallace, a loyal Federalist. Everybody thought it was a great joke.

I kind of liked it, too, until I found out why they called it Braddock's Field. The famous British general had been there during the French and Indian War.

And been disastrously and gorily defeated.

14

The Spirit of '94

JULY 31, 1794

"Taxation is theft!"

The Indian pony danced, rearing to its hind legs and snorting emotional, if not philosophical agreement as its rider brandished a feather-decorated tomahawk in the middle of Pittsburgh's only cobbled street.

"It ain't just the excise law that's gotta go down," the rider bellowed. *"That ain't all I want, not by a long shot! Your district an' associate judges gotta go down, their high offices an' salaries. I ain't even started yet! A lot more's gonna get done! Death to the Federalists! Death an' destruction!"*

Along the wooden sidewalks, conventionally dressed passersby shrank to the storefronts, with their imported glass-paned windows. Matrons shrieked and seized their children, holding them as they squirmed against the folds of their voluminous skirts. Here and there, an occasional cheer was heard. When people turned to stare, its origin had vanished. A young girl fluttered her lashes and swooned, offering her beau a purely medicinal opportunity to chafe her wrists or take other, more daring liberties.

"Remember the Alamo—uh, make that Bunker Hill! C'mon, Tony, let's skedaddle!" Displaying the yellow arm-band beginning to be associated with the Rebellion, the buckskinned interloper wheeled the pinto, dashed up the street, and repeated the performance for another appreciative audience. History was in the making. Today was the first day of the Second Revolution. Yet a century from now, no historian would be able to name its rustically clad herald. She hadn't even left a silver bullet.

Beside me on the boardwalk, Hugh Henry Brackenridge shivered. "...it is indeed to be revolution, then, organized and managed upon Jacobin principles. My friend—" he turned to the only unpreoccupied face in the crowd—yours truly's "—I recently penned a bit of doggerel in jest, commemorating events in France, that began 'Louis Capet has lost his caput'..."

The ongoing French revolution was all the rage here, as well as in the rest of the United States. France's Citizen Ambassador Edmond Genet was on a triumphant multicity speaking tour—later he'd be invited back home to his own guillotining and would become America's first applicant for political asylum. Brackenridge glanced up the street where the tomahawk rider had fired shots into the air—seven of them—and disappeared. He fingered his bullish neck. "It was published in the *Pittsburgh Gazette.* Now I must confess that I can scarcely bear to cast my eye over a paragraph of French news."

Laughing, I clapped him on the back. "You know how it is, Hugh Henry: 'the guilty flee where no man pursueth.'" His mouth dropped open and he stared at me. I took the cigar out of his hand, relit the clay pipe I'd acquired at one of the local emporia, then gave it back, turned on my heel, and insinuated myself into the crowd, leaving the guy who was the original prototype for expressions about "Philadelphia lawyers" to quiver in my wake. There were a thousand stories in the naked city.

I moccasined my way up the boardwalk, calabash in hand and my eyes and ears wide open. Fashionably attired citizens avoided contact with my greasy leathers. It made me feel like Marlon Brando's motorcycle mechanic.

I was here in Pittsburgh, doing the job I was best suited for: detective work. For the benefit of her academic clients, Ooloorie had asked us to track down a smear-story to the effect that British soldiers had been spotted among the "rioters" gathering in Braddock's Field. We couldn't turn her down: those clients were paying for this expedition. The bit with the pony and the tomahawk had been suggested to sort of focus public awareness. The rumor wasn't altogether baseless. There had been general speculation about rejoining the Empire back toward the beginning of the Rebellion. The Brits had outposts west of the Appalachians. Arms and ammunition might be obtained from sympathetic Canadians, and so forth, and so on. But it was silly-talk, cast more in ironic tones—"What did we fight the

Revolution for, anyway?"—than in any real serious-
ness. These frontier people were more *American* in
attitude than any of the Anglophilic gang that had con-
spired to pass the excise laws. For that matter there'd
been discussion about starting a new state, though what
good that would do where a nationwide tax was involved
was beyond me.

I had my own ideas about that rumor. Philadelphia-
ward, the malignant spirit of Alexander Hamilton
loomed like a spectre. This story felt like his handi-
work. As an idle student of *The Federalist Papers*,
written by the Secretary and his buddies to justify the
bloodless counterrevolution the Constitution represented, I knew reabsorption by the Crown had been
one threat a vigorous central government was designed
to preclude. His propaganda pieces also mentioned
predations by Native Americans, war between the
States (which the Constitution had failed to prevent in
my time-line), uniform, reliable currency—a sort of
ultimate sick-joke—and, if alien saucer invasions had
been in the eighteenth-century vocabulary, he'd have
thrown them in for good measure. Bogeymen were
something Hamilton was conversant with, having been
one for a long time, himself.

I wandered through the crowd, just one of many
tourists visiting the wicked city. Locals complained
that strangers were hanging out in the streets, sniffing
around Fort Fayette like spies. It was circus-day, all
right. An impressive number of country folk were
bringing their produce to market, offering it at bargain
rates for flints and powder. A lot of blacksmiths found

themselves doing a land-office business repairing old guns.

I stopped at a wooden Indian, relit my pipe at the glass-encased candle it was holding, and began to seek some privacy. I never could keep a pipe going at the best of times, and it was getting to be a nuisance in a culture that hadn't invented matches. Twenty minutes later, flies buzzed around my head as I occupied an overpriced, underluxuried one-holer behind Pittsburgh's only commercial bath-o-mat. In the stuffy semidarkness provided by a crescent-shaped ventilator, I shifted on the planking, wondering whether the traditional decoration reflected deep-buried anti-Moslem tendencies in Christian culture.

"...add to that, the fact that the public's being uncooperative, as usual. It's like being a play-producer, hanging around the lobby at intermission, when all the audience wants to talk about is what was on TV last night." In the field of vision provided by my skinsuit hood floated the deceptively smiling features of Ooloorie Eckickeck P'wheet, being transmitted from the Emperor Norton University in whatever the twenty-second-century had left of San Francisco.

"Tell me, landling, what you *have* managed to discover, then."

"Sure." I ignored the implication of my incompetence. She was like that: anybody provided with toes and fingers didn't need to think, couldn't possess the intellectual capabilities of a sea-slug. "There's plenty of gossip in the streets, take your pick, most of it related to the latest fashions, depressingly concealing; what's going on in Paris, beheadings by the basketful; the price of crops, never high enough to satisfy farmers; and, as always, who's bundling with who."

"Whom."

"All right, get touchy on me. What useful scuttlebutt I've separated out amounts to this: one, no mention of British soldiers, starting a new state, *or* invasions from Mars—"

"Invasions from Mars?" Paddling her flippers in the water, Ooloorie wrinkled her forehead, an expression she's acquired from humans.

Encased in dirty buckskins, I suppressed the urge to spend the next several hours scratching. "Never mind. Two, somebody named James Ross, along with other 'levelheaded' citizens, is trying to persuade David Bradford and James Marshall, now viewed as the leading insurrectionists, to 'spare Pittsburgh' in exchange for placing Abraham Kirkpatrick, Presley Neville, General John Gibson, James Brison, Edward Day, and Thomas Butler in a sort of exile. The townsmen will then march out onto Braddock's Field the next day to display their solidarity with the rebels."

Ooloorie sighed. "Humans." Absently, she caught a herring swimming by and munched it down. "How much of this solidarity is there?"

"Ooloorie, there're thousands of armed insurgents gathered outside the city. Pittsburgh's self-appointed civic leaders are pretending to be wheeling and dealing with the rebels, while remaining sympathetic with the government's excise laws. The average guy's burying his savings, silverware, and family heirlooms in his backyard—protecting them from *whom*, I don't think even he's sure."

She made sympathetic noises. "I remember reading about that."

"Well," I said, "it's an old story. I just hadn't realized how old. Like that amnesty of Brackenridge's. Somehow, this revolution's been turned on its own tail, becoming a matter of people versus people, instead of all the people versus the real enemy of peace, progress, and prosperity everywhere. Go figure it."

"Machinations at the top?"

"That's what you commissioned me to find out. Sorry, from here I just don't know. But unless somebody does something fast, the Rebellion will be lost before it's begun—which is what happened in my home time-line."

"That somebody will have to be Albert Gallatin," Ooloorie said.

Which brought my mind around to Ed. While Lucy and I were otherwise occupied in Pittsburgh, he and Ochskahrt had been shadowing the Swiss country gentleman, who'd responded to the Braddock's Field militia call along with five or six thousand other local inhabitants.

"Edna can strike at any time, Ooloorie, but our plan is still not to meet the old fellow—I still think of him that way, from images on coins, I guess, despite the fact he's just thirty-three years old at the moment. We'll just unobtrusively watch his back."

The fishy scientist nodded. "If things go right, he'll never know it's being done. If they go wrong," added the cynical cetacean, "he'll never know that, either."

I glanced at my wristwatch, discovered it wasn't there this century, decided it wasn't worth messing with my skinsuit-instruments to find out the exact time. I rose. "Thanks for the vote of confidence. I'll begin elbowing my way through the crowd toward the end of town nearest Braddock's Field. I'm late already. It's my turn to mind the baby, while Ed plays Philip Marlowe for you."

We signed off. I peeled down my hood, tucked it into the neck of my shirt, opened the door, and stepped out through the buzzing of the flies, back into the sunlight.

I ran into Lucy, right on schedule, as I was down the street arranging for a horse.

"Lookie here, you simpering cephaloplegic!" One hand managing her extra skirt-yardage, she shook a scrawny fist, her face screwed into its own center like a dried-up apple. It was hot in the rough plank building, over a sort of olfactory bass-note of horse droppings, the baritone of burning hardwood and tenor of hot metal filling the air. For the moment, though, the percussion section—blacksmith's hammer—was silent. He was occupied with other, more pressing business.

Lucy said: "We're gonna settle this account, here an' now, *macho a macho*, or I'm gonna know the reason why!" She'd changed back into eighteenth-century feminine attire. Now she was trying, without success, to settle the rental on the pony. The stableman, an overmuscled, sweaty specimen with a singed ponytail, had his thighlike arms folded across his grimy leather apron, a grim, unforgiving expression on his unshaven face—mixed with a glint of avarice in his small, piggish eyes. He rumbled, "A bargain, madame, is a bargain."

Putting a hand on Lucy's shoulder I asked, "'Cephaloplegic'?"

She jumped, then turned to me. "Somebody paralyzed from the neck up—" She whirled back to the blacksmith. "An' don't you dast commence that 'madame' business again, you misbegotten iron-pumper. We had ourselves a deal, ordinary day-rates. What I done with the horse, long as I brought her back healthy, ain't none of your nevermind!"

The horse-renter's eyebrows shot up. He reached into an apron pocket, smiled, produced the feathered tomahawk, holding it up for inspection. "But you see, madame, there must be an additional price, for public sedition, payable by the authorities—once defaulted upon by the traitor."

Tie a Yellow Ribbon

The blacksmith took a step forward, another sideways, stretched a stubby hand in the direction of the hammer lying across the anvil.

Licking my thumb, I ran it along the front sight of my rifle, raised the weapon to port, and drawled, "I wouldn't try that, friend." I don't know what that bit's supposed to accomplish, but it looks neat. Glancing at Lucy, I added, "Man gets upset when you hit his mother on the hand with a hammer."

"Sure t'leave a bad impression on her mind," she responded, hitching her skirt. There was a surprise there for the stableman—fourteen of them—if she could get at it. I caught a glint of metal in my peripheral vision. She had both seven-shooters trained on him.

The larcenous horse-trader swiveled his fire-hydrant neck, looking from one of us to the other. He decided we meant it, started an angry expression on his broad

127

grimy face, then converted it to resignation. He let his racket-sized hand drop and backed away from the anvil. No armistice, just a cease-fire.

I sidestepped away from the door toward a wall, not liking empty space behind my back. As I did, the doorway darkened. I lowered my rifle, letting it rest on its curved brass recoil-pad. Lucy's pistols disappeared. A pair of well-dressed Pittsburghers entered, interrupting our business conference with the request that the horses they boarded be readied for a ride to Braddock's Field. The unkempt proprietor nodded, going along with the masquerade, began hollering orders.

An undernourished pimple-face materialized to carry them out. Grabbing a double armful of posterior-polished leather, he dragged it toward the stalls at the back. The boss stood around, kicking straw and grunting commonplaces with the clientele—while keeping one suspicious eye over their shoulders on my aged mother. Who stood fuming and speechless.

In the interim, I'd had time for thought. My waistband held another handkerchief like the one worn by the mysterious tomahawk-wielder. I extracted it from beneath my homespun, wadding the cheap material in my fist. Pretending to examine some horse-tackle on the wall, I watched the owner in a reflective bit-escutcheon, his attention divided between Lucy and his clients. When he turned to bellow his assistant up to a higher velocity, I stashed the yellow band in the bottom of a feed-bag firebranded house property.

I turned. Horses had been brought out. The customers were being waited on. Now the proprietor had time for us again. Lucy didn't wait for the others to leave before she was back to haggling. "This here's blackmail, an' you know it!"

The blacksmith smiled, displaying black gaps in his brown teeth. "Madame, be so good as to lower your voice, unless you want the accusation leveled here and now, to nobody's profit." He tossed a glance toward his clients, climbing aboard their animals.

Rifle in hand, I stepped up to him. "Look here, stablekeeper, blackmail is a two-way street."

"A two-way street?" Puzzlement furrowed his forge-darkened features. "Pray tell what street is *not* a two-way street? Wherever do you come by such a peculiar phrase?"

I blew air through my nose, grounded the rifle, put a hand on my Bowie-pommel, and started again. "I mean sedition is like witchcraft. Anyone can accuse anyone else and make the charge stick. Take it from an excop—er, make that former constable, and... what's that, Lucy? Oh all right, Goddamn it, town *marshall*, then." I stopped to catch my breath. The man's eyes had widened at the casual blasphemy, lowering my opinion of local blacksmiths. "My mother has paid you your due. Take it while you can." He started to interrupt. I didn't let him. Thumping him with each word in that tender spot between the collarbones, I warned, "You whisper a word of this to anyone, and I'll produce uncontrovertible proof that you yourself are one of Tom the Tinker's men."

"G'wan!" he sneered. "There's no such—"

"I know there's evidence," I told him. "I planted it here, while you were busy with the paying customers."

He opened his mouth. He shut it.
We left.

Tenting tonight,
Tenting tonight,
Tenting on the old campground.

Braddock's Field lay eight miles outside the city, below where Turtle Creek joined the Monongahela, an open plain along the eastern bank. Getting here, the back-country militia had crossed a ford used by Braddock's ill-fated army ascending through cuts made by British engineers for their wheeled ordnance. In 1794, the place was used for horse-pasture. Farther from the river, the ground became hilly, serrated by ravines, wooded.

Five thousand unmilitary beings were sandwiched into the place, cheek-to-figurative-cheek, in an area not much larger than a football stadium. There was canvas everywhere—guy-ropes a positive menace to navigation—and a constant ground-fog of campfire smoke we came to be grateful for, owing to a proliferation of unwashed humanity and their equine mass-transit, or rather the road-pollution it was leaving behind. The spectacle resembled a mismanaged scout jamboree, complete with oversized boys and underqualified counselors. Drill teams with mismatched firearms and clothing hup-hoop-heeped across hill and dale, led by volunteer captains with generals' stars in their eyes. The sloppy columns often ran smack into each other like rehearsing contingents of Keystone Kops. Disorganized confusion was the rule, just like in Pittsburgh at the moment, but in the Braddock's Field encampment, on a more ambitious scale. Incidental street-talk was another difference: Alexander Hamilton—what he would persuade the President to do—was the unspoken subject of every conversation.

It took Lucy and me an hour to find the Confederate contingent. Safe inside our tent, we reported camp news to Ed, who'd taken my place in the city. Ochskahrt was laced up inside his sleeping bag, playing "Beautiful Dreamer."

"—riel Blakeney," I was saying into my suit-face, passing on a tidbit we'd picked up, "and William Meetkirk, prominent citizens, also Absalom Baird—he was the guy who ordered Lenox's arrest—have agreed to transmit rebel terms to the Pittsburgh town meeting called to deal with the emergency. They'll accept Pittsburgh's offer to exile the Federalists and return the mail we went to all that trouble stealing."

"*Shhh!*" Lucy protested, "the walls have ears!" She stopped, scratched beneath her short ribs. "Or something, anyway."

"—ugly catch—" Ed telepathized, taking a break from his legwork for a quick bite of jerky near the wooden Indian I'd made acquaintance with. "—is that they're to be interviewed at this end by Wallace, Brackenridge, and John Wilkins, Junior—Pittsburgh's leading fencestraddlers—with Presley Neville present and John Gibson presiding." He paused. "Oh, yes. There's been an additional development. It's being announced that a 'Committee of Twenty-one' has taken over city government for the duration..."

He panned along the street for our benefit. Town criers were doing the announcing, others nailed up printed handbills. People sniggered: another committee.

"A peculiar coup d'etat," my look-alike commented, "leaving the same city-hall loafers in control as the day before—reorganized so none of them have to take individual responsibility for what comes next: asking Mssrs. Kirkpatrick, Brison, Day, and the rest to 'absent themselves for the good of all.' No one can quite summon up the courage to brace Gibson and Presley about leaving." An eerie electronic chuckle issued from his implant. "Gossip has it that the situation wasn't even mentioned to them—until Henry Purviance, one of the committee, insisted." He laughed. "The Committee spent a good deal of time adopting a swell-sounding resolution for the benefit of Braddock's Field, to be printed both as newspaper ad and handbill. It's already leaked all over the place."

"Here, too," Lucy offered. "John Scull, of the *Pittsburgh Gazette*, demonstratin' a cynicism I didn't know'd already developed in his profession, plans t'labor through the night typesettin' the Committee's pretense that they're entrenched against the excise."

"You should hear Brackenridge: 'Pittsburgh's rebellious sons will be represented at Braddock's Field on the morrow.'" Ed snorted. "And they want to come to Parkinson's Ferry!"

I laughed. Outside, an increase in the genreal clamor caused me to peel my face and peek out through the flaps into the failing light. Fife, drums, and the *squish, squish, squishity* of feet stomping out of time. Up and down the muddy avenues between the tents, David Bradford, dressed in a bright, custom-tailored generalissimo's outfit, complete with a feathery cocked hat and enough brass buttons to cast small cannon from, was giving his troops a series of drills. I hadn't known District Attorneys had troops. Was everybody in this century crazy?

Not quite. When I replaced my face-piece, Ed was watching a young family of Pittsburghers out in their yard. Mama held a lamp, swatting away the moths it was beginning to draw; Papa made with a shovel—the kids were busy sounding out a handbill stuck to one of their trees, promising Peace In Our Time—burying their valuables.

16
Rain of Terror

AUGUST 2, 1794

"Aaaachooo!"

An old familiar tension braiding my insides, I hunched in the midnight mist, a sheet of oily latigo turning to soup around me while it failed to protect me from the drizzle. I had a case of stake-out jitters, telling me that tonight was the night.

Suppressing a second sneeze, I half leaned on my rifle, checking the fit of the rawhide muzzle-cover. And the priming pan for the ten-thousandth time. It made an individual appreciate the nineteenth century and self-contained metallic cartridges. What I wouldn't have given for a .45 Peacemaker or a lever-action Winchester. "Keep your powder dry" was more than just an idle turn of phrase in the 1700s; it was a way of life. One hoped.

I shivered, wanting a cigar I couldn't have—the

glow would give me away, and it was too wet—wishing I could send my nerves back on warranty. Something important was about to happen. Judging from the centipedes rappelling down the back of my neck, it wasn't going to be nice.

It really was a dark and stormy night, overcast and moonless. An occasional third-rate lightning flicker gave me tachistoscopic glimpses of endless badly ordered tent rows stretching across the muddy plain to the Monongahela. In view of my earlier illness, Ed had cautioned me to wake him if it began precipitating in earnest, but I hadn't. There's that streak in all men that resents being mentioned in the same context as poultry excretion. No dignity, calling in sick in a life-and-death situation, however circumspect it may be.

Now, however, as the chill seeped deeper and the apprehension built itself inside me for no intelligent reason I could think of—except my long experience as a minion of the law—I was beginning to regret not having dragged him out. Oh well, he was due to relieve me in another soggy hour or so. Let the poor slob sleep. Maybe he and Lucy had found some place that was dry.

Don't get me wrong. There was some joy in what was rapidly becoming Mudville, would have been boisterous, whiskey-powered celebration, if it hadn't been for the weather. That afternoon, before the rain, breathless reports had arrived of outbreaks against the excise in the Shenandoah Valley. Kirkpatrick and Brison had been seen skulking out of Pittsburgh, the first of the Federalist exiles to do so. Intelligence (Ed, poking around the city) suggested that General Wilkins

had received an emergency order from Governor Mifflin to bring us rioters to swift, stern justice. I'd have
guessed that to be Thomas Butler's job—never did get
protocol straight. In any event, Wilkins had acted with
prompt decision—by hiding the order. His father, a
Pittsburgh merchant, was coming out in a day or so to
talk us out of burning his establishment to the ground.
Fine. Nobody'd thought of doing such a thing until he
suggested it.

The Rebellion seemed to be getting somewhere.

So why the willy-fidgets on my part? For one thing,
I needed to go to the bathroom—a mile across the
rain-drenched field to the river, another mile in the
dark, downstream, to keep things sanitary. Ed wouldn't
be here to let me off the hook for another long hour.
For another, while everybody else was logging down-
time, I was stuck in the rain, guarding Albert Gallatin's
tent, trying not to be conspicuous, and sort of resenting
the fact that Edna hadn't had the courtesy to show up.
So far. And for another—

"Monsieur?"

"GHAAA!!" I jumped three feet when the hand
clamped on my shoulder, whirled, heart pounding, my
own sweaty digits on the handle of my Bowie. I followed the intruding appendage up as it became a lace-
decorated wrist, a silk-encased forearm, a stylish
elbow . . . At its other end was a neat, small-framed,
gentle-looking specimen, with twinkling gray eyes
behind thick spectacles, an ironic twist of a smile, and
even less hair than Ochskahrt made a habit of wearing.
He'd even thought to bring an umbrella.

"Beg pardon, *Monsieur* Bear, for startling you . . ."

I goggled: with his other hand, he offered me a steaming mug of coffee. "... but I came, *mon ami*, to inquire, since you have taken it upon yourself to guard my life, will you not at least come in where it is warm and dry—" He held the canopy over my waterlogged brains. I took a deep, grateful gulp of the near-boiling liquid. "—*and tell me why the hell you are doing it?*"

Oil lamps flickered, casting grotesque shadows on canvas. Somebody was going to have to loosen up the stake-ropes when—and if—the weather brightened, or this place was going to tear itself in half.

I poured another cup of coffee, felt at the cuffs of my long woolen underwear to see if it was drying on the line we'd suspended between two poles, checked the buckskins, too, hung to prevent frontier sanfori-zation, further from the fire, near the entrance. Bone-weary, I lowered myself onto a folding Army cot I hadn't known had been invented already—by the Romans. My skinsuit was doing a nice job of warming me up under the colorful trading blanket that concealed it. Given time, it would leach fatigue-acids out of my sore muscles. It was even managing to correct my fluid balance, so the pressure on my bladder had eased for the moment.

Security was provided by my Heller Effect Kentucky, wiped spotless and leaning against the cot-frame with a dry charge of pan-powder. My host favored a brace of horse-pistols, backed up by the good offices of an enormous Negro sitting just inside the doorflap with what must have been a two-gauge shotgun lying across his lap. The servant, introduced as Cato, assisted me in lowering the coffee-level again. Already we'd had sizzling bacon, hardtack with bacon gravy, and something reminiscent of chutney. After the chill outside, this was paradise. If Ed wanted to sleep in, that was his bad luck.

The boss held a hand up, palm out, when I offered to warm up his cup, too. I shook my head and grinned, at the brevity of my tenure as an inconspicuous bodyguard.

Unlike most Presidents, Gallatin hadn't changed the course of history by being stupid. Of course, he wasn't President yet; maybe that made a difference. Whatever the reason, he'd caught me by surprise out there in the rain—the drizzle had become a downpour, so the guy whose life I was supposed to be preserving had probably saved mine. As we talked, he continued surprising me.

"*Mais oui*, to be certain, I have followed your progress and that of your companions—your friend who looks like you, the lady who is not your mother, and the fellow with the violoncello who has the wrong German accent to be Pennsylvania *Deutsch*—since you arrived in Washington County."

What was I supposed to say? I glanced at where my watch should have been—Ed was getting later and later—and made the appropriate reply, none at all.

Gallatin smiled. "Deception is the order of the day. You are not the only dissembling strangers here, my friend." He leaned back, stretching a knickered leg. His knee-britches ended not with stockings and silver-buckled slippers, but at the stitch-rolled edges of a pair of heavy boots. Brushing aside his many-buttoned coat, he fished in a vest pocket, extracting a wad of paper. "Have you seen these handbills distributed among our battalions to lubricate the entrance of the Committee of Twenty-one?"

It was hard to tell if he'd intended it. There always seemed to be a Gallic twinkle in his eye that gave away his ancestry long before his Jacques Cousteau accent did. I liked his choice of metaphor. The Pittsburgh expedition had left the city about ten the previous morning, in the racket of fife and drum that accompanied everything around here. By the time they'd arrived at Braddock's Field two hours later, handbills or not, they'd managed to make the opposite kind of stir they'd hoped for.

"We 'rebels' are not fooled." Gallatin lit a long clay pipe. Cato had a pipe of his own. I dug out a dampened cigar. "An acquaintance informs me that *Monsieur* Brackenridge, this . . . this *lawyer* who imagines himself among the *literati*, already sketches our historic gathering for a book he plans to write . . ."

If I was supposed to say something here, I didn't know what, so I kept my mouth shut and concentrated on controlling a bladder that was demanding attention again.

"He will say—" The former Harvard professor, economist, historian, philosopher, linguist, ethnographer, future Secretary of the Treasury (in another universe), future President (in this one), laughed. "—that we ignorant frontiersmen '. . . discussed our grievances in the half-mute, half-profane language of the common man . . .'"

I shook my head. "He thinks himself one of the aristocracy."

"A new aristocracy," Gallatin replied, "of lawyers." He changed his mind about the coffee, poured out the last drops. "Have we no more to drink, then, Cato?"

The black man didn't take his eyes off the crack between the tent-flaps. "I'll hafta go for more water, Mr. Gallatin. Should I do that?"

Gallatin looked at me. "Sir, thus far you have evaded my questioning, but you shall not Cato's. Is it safe for him to go for water?"

I grinned—getting to be a habit in Gallatin's presence. "For him, maybe. Not for you. Go ahead, Cato, we've got enough hardware to protect us a few minutes."

Gallatin slapped his thigh. "Now that I have got it started, the remainder of this conversation should prove enlightening. Hurry, Cato, your opinion will be solicited." Shouldering canvas aside, Cato ducked into the deluge, enameled coffeepot in one hand, monster shotgun in the other. Gallatin puckered his eyebrows at me. "Well, *monsieur*?"

I gave him the edited version, leaving out the twenty-second century, time-travel, laser pistols. Ed, Lucy, and I believed he was the man to straighten this mess out. Also, we knew the opposition agreed and were inclined to do something ugly about it. I made short work of it; shorn of futuristic trappings, there wasn't much to tell. I was also worrying about my partner—and the coffee having its way with me. I wished Cato would get back and keep an eye on his boss so I could take a walk.

Gallatin gave me an odd look now and again, especially in the blue-penciled areas. "Secretary Hamilton I do not like. Nor his policies. This he knows—I was elected to the national legislature, then expelled by his, how you say, cronies? On a technicality—my length of residence."

I nodded. There'd been something of a public scandal.

"Now you say I must assume leadership of an insurrection! *Mon dieu!* They were right, in their way, to exclude me. I am a stranger to these shores, having come but nine years ago. I did not fight the Revolution, though I admire those who did—it is why I came. I do not know the country, its civilization well enough—things puzzle me..."

"They puzzle everybody, Mr. Gallatin." I relit my cigar; it was still damp and kept going out. "What things puzzle you?"

"Well, for example..." He rummaged in his baggage, found a well-worn book. "The words of Thomas Jefferson: if government prove unsatisfactory, it ought to be replaced—by 'new guards for our future security'—because it has not been operating by 'the unanimous consent of the governed.'" He pronounced that last with three syllables.

"Sure," I agreed, "the Declaration of Independence. What puzzles you about that?"

He held the book out. "Look here." It was written in German, published in Geneva. Gallatin handled all four languages of his native country, plus what Lucy would call a passle of others. "If it were not for that one little word... I have been given a new home, welcomed by people who built this country. But I am, how you say, *nagged* by that one little word..."

Two syllables that time: nag-ged. I thought I knew what he meant. Better to let him reason it out himself. If I was right, this wasn't a moment to mess with. "Which one is that?"

"'Unanimous'—'... the unanimous consent of the governed.' Hamilton swears it is meaningless rhetoric. Jefferson maintains it is up to the Congress who ratified it. I know the word. This encampment is evidence unanimity does not exist, at least where taxes are concerned."

"Sounds like a legal matter to me. What do the lawyers say?"

"That my concerns are frivolous. Impractical. Nothing could ever be accomplished by the State under such restraints." He frowned. "Perhaps that is the very reason for its inclusion!"

I laughed. "It precludes the tyranny imposed by Philadelphia!"

"*Monsieur*, the lawyers I know locally are from Pittsburgh. They come, they tour our camp, they lie about commitment to our cause. This evening, having failed to convince anyone, on the excuse that they have brought no food, they decide to return home." He laughed this time. "A fearful Brackenridge talked them out of this transparent confession. He thinks we intend destruction of the town—some few rebels wish it, out of envy for civic prosperity—having estimated our strength, the committee would now go home to fortify against the onslaught."

Onslaught and a half. Estimates of the gathering

varied, I knew, from Gallatin's of fifteen hundred—half again the population of Pittsburgh itself—to Wilkins's of five or six thousand. He may have been right, with a military man's experience at sizing up the enemy. It was impossible to tell, between weather and disorder. Brackenridge, seeing Tom the Tinker under every bed, put the number at seven thousand. I was glad I didn't dream *his* dreams.

Gallatin ruminated, while I wondered where the hell Ed was—and if Cato was ever coming back. I'm suggestible where certain things are concerned, and the rain was driving me crazy.

"Thank you, *Monsieur* Bear," Gallatin said at last, "for your inestimable advice. I have made up my mind." He patted a breast pocket. Paper crackled. I felt a thrill crawl down my spine. "I have drafted a proposal . . . now I shall offer it, first thing tomor—"

There was a thump outside. The doorflaps were parted by a rolling projectile. Into our midst tumbled a ten-pound wooden powder keg, its quick-burning fuse down to the last two inches!

17

The Bombs of
August

I did the only thing I could. The fuse got put out. That's
all I'm going to say.

Gathering weapons, Gallatin and I poked cautious
heads outside. The downpour had become a torrent (if
there's a difference), with visibility down to about three
feet. I tripped over something—or it tripped over me.
"Unghh!"

"Edward William Bear, I presume," said the mud-
covered lump, "fancy meeting you here."

"Edward William Bear yourself," I answered, also
coated with liquid topsoil. "We've got to stop meeting
like this—where the bloody hell have you been?"

He raised an unrecognizable face toward me and
hissed. "What the Congress do you mean where have
I been? You called and told me to meet you at Bradford's tent, so I—"

"Edna." We said it together.

Gallatin bent over us, pistol in one hand, umbrella in the other, his second gun ruining the waistband of his tailored knee-trousers. "Gentlemen, gentlemen!" He waved his arms. "I implore you! Cato should have been back long ago! Please help me look for him."

In the end, it was Lucy who found him, after Ed contacted her and Ochskahrt via implant. The bunch of us were bumbling through the tent-clotted field. When we responded to her angry paratronic shout, it came from down by the river. Cato lay on the muddy stream-bank, his undischarged shotgun beside him. No sign of the coffeepot, it had been replaced by a stainless-steel knife. Protruding from his back.

"Don't move him!" Lucy still shouted, to be heard over the rain. "I dunno how, but he's alive!" She bent over, did things with the pockets of her suit, then placed a hand around the handle of the weapon. There wasn't any blade showing.

Gallatin stepped forward. "Don't—"

I took his arm. "Trust her, sir. She knows what she's doing."

With a grunt, she drew the knife out, placed something over the wound, laid a hand on Cato's forehead, closed her eyes. It must have looked like faith-healing.

"Okay." She stood, gestured to the rest of us for help. "We can move him now—but easy!"

"What a peculiar knife," Gallatin observed. Someone had to cover us while we were encumbered. The honor had gone to him and Lucy. Ed took Cato's shoulders, and Ochskahrt and I took his feet.

Gallatin had accepted the weapon from Lucy, looking it over as he strode beside us, one eye on the landscape. Its metal handle consisted of two parallel hollow bars hinge-pinned to the blade-base, each with a row of decorative holes. A latch at the pommel kept the bars together. Lucy took it, snicked the latch off with her little finger, gave the whole contraption a graceful circular flip. The swiveling five-inch blade seemed to vanish, tucked away between the handle-halves. She brushed the latch shut on a thigh to keep it closed.

"A balisong," I told the future President. Lucy had surprised me. Butterfly daggers were a kind of concealable defense the gun-happy Confederacy hadn't found necessary to invent. "They won't be introduced in America until—"

"*Win!*"

I craned around to return Ed's glare. "What do you want?"

"Your help. Watch where you're going. Let's get Cato inside." Ochskahrt chose that moment to slip and fall, face-first, making it *three* Abominable Mudmen.

Thanks to Gallatin's solicitous concern, Cato's innate toughness, and twenty-second-century first aid, the black man lived. It's harder to kill with a knife than people expect—that's why stabbing-murders are so grisly. You slide your Boy Scout folder into somebody's gizzard, the victim keeps wiggling around yelling. One stab calls for another, and before you know

it, you're one of those seventy-four-wound killers people read about in the tabloids. Yech.

Next morning dawned clear and bright. Leaving Cato
to the care of Lucy, Gallatin met the joint chiefs of this
Chinese fire drill with the declared object of forming
yet another committee. I was sick of the word. This
particular body of men entirely surrounded by bullshit
would consist of three lucky souls elected by each
volunteer battalion. Its purpose would be to adopt a
plan of action for the day.

For the day! Was this any way to run a revolution?

Pittsburgh was represented by Wilkins, Captain John
M'Masters, and Hugh Henry Brackenridge, who moved
that the committee take itself some distance into the
woods, "in order that they might be undisturbed in their
deliberations." A swell opening gambit, but it didn't
work. Soon as the committee-members began strolling
across the field, a crowd of curious rank-and-file, sens-
ing steamrollers in the wind, began to follow them. It
got to be quite a parade.

Once there, Edward Cook was elected chairman,
requesting that nonmembers vamoose. Some few were
polite enough to do so. Other, more cynical types soon
took their place. Our "secret conference" wound up
being held before a gallery of the most radical and
suspicious curmudgeons in the camp. Lucy would have
felt right at home. New battalions were arriving at
Braddock's Field every hour. Once plugged in, they'd
send even more delegates—and peanut gallerites.

Bradford opened by stating that the purpose, not of
this committee meeting, but of the general mayhem out
in the field was to identify and punish individuals

friendly to the excise. This was news to those who'd
showed up to do something about the excise itself. To
provide examples, Bradford read the letters we'd taken
and mentioned Major Isaac Craig, John Neville's son-
in-law, whom he accused of intending to open a tax-
inspection office in his own house to replace the one
closed down in Pittsburgh. The Pittsburghers denied
it.

Brackenridge's turn arrived. He tried to divert the
wrath of the insurgents from the Major by ridiculing
him. The last time he'd run into Craig, he'd passed
along a rumor (made up on the spot) that the rebels
had found old cannon at the bottom of the river, left
by Braddock, and were hauling them up to use on the
fort. Brackenridge got some mileage describing the
major's panic, but not enough to change what was going
on in the clearing.

Bradford got impatient. "Enough of your droll stories, sir. I tell you, the people came out to do something, and something they must do. On that account,
I suggest we dispose of the men under censure by
taking each one up individually."

That suited everybody. Butler and Craig being army
officers, their dismissal should be demanded of the
Secretary of War. Gibson and Presley should be ban-
ished. And so on and so on. Ochskahrt sat on the
ground across the clearing, cradling his beloved cello
between his knees. Ed and I found a fallen log that
wasn't too damp, on the perimeter of the shifting ring
of spectators, among a dozen riflemen leaning on their
rifles, and listened. We looked at each other, shook

our heads, and shrugged. We'd both had experience with politics. This didn't look any different.

As the high school forensics dragged on, I watched Ed get more and more restless. He stood, elbowed his way through the Daniel Boone impersonators, and strode forward. "Gentlemen, we 'simple folk' do not understand your counseling in secrecy. Do something speedily. Or we shall go and do something ourselves."

That got some attention—the delegates went into something resembling shock. Good heavens, if the battalions decided to march without official policy, there was no telling what might happen. Like when they reached Pittsburgh. You could see it written on Brackenridge's pudgy face.

Moving to regain leadership, David Bradford opened his mouth. And closed it again. Gallatin had risen to speak.

"My friends, I hesitate to criticize neighbors who offered refuge to a stranger on these shores. Thus I have been reluctant to participate in events that call us together." There was muttering from the spectators. It sounded like more talk to them. "But the question has been asked. I must reply with all the frankness I can muster. To do less would be disservice to those good neighbors."

He looked at David Bradford. "Tom the Tinker's men, my friends, have erred from the first, making enemies on every side through threats of what would happen should they comply with the excise or fail to join in rebellion."

He peered at Brackenridge over the rims of his glasses. "Now, as one consequence, claim is being made that everybody in this rebellion rises only out of fear of everybody else! Thus the bizarre misimpression that we rebel, not against the excise and the government, but because our neighbors are brutes—and we ourselves cowards!"

Angry, confused reactions from committee and spectators alike. Gallatin, voice thin and accent thick, managed to shout them down. "Consider *Monsieur* Brackenridge, *mes amis*. In the event of defeat, if he and the other—'fence-sitters' inform Hamilton that they came to Braddock's Field out of fear for their lives, they cannot reasonably be prosecuted for attempting to overthrow the State."

He fumbled in his jacket. "I have prepared a document that will draw lines between those who resist the government in this matter and those who support it in suppressing their neighbors. Moreover—" Several attempted interruptions. Many here didn't want that line drawn. "*Moreover*, albeit I make no comparisons to, for example, the Magna Carta, or the Declaration of Independence—even to the Constitution that brought us to this pass—I believe this document will assure that something like this can happen never again.

"Therefore, *mes amis*, I, Abraham Alfonse Albert Gallatin, propose: *A New Covenant, among the Individual Inhabitants of the Continent of North America*—"

There were mutters from the crowd. Gallatin adjusted his spectacles. "We, the undersigned Witnesses to the Lesson of History—that no Form of political Governance may be relied upon to secure the individual Rights of Life, Liberty, or Property—now therefore establish and provide certain fundamental Precepts measuring our Conduct toward one another, and toward others:"

Beside me, one of the men murmured, "What in the name of what a bear does in the woods does that mean?"

"That democracy hasn't worked," Ed whispered, "and Gallatin wants to try something else."

"Oh."

"First," Gallatin continued, not having heard the whispers, "that we shall henceforward recognize each Individual to be the exclusive Proprietor of his or her own Existence and of all Products of that Existence, holding no Obligation binding among Individuals excepting those to which they voluntarily and explicitly consent;

"Second," said Gallatin, "that under no Circumstances shall we acknowledge any Liberty to initiate Force against another person, and shall instead defend the inalienable Right of Individuals to resist Coercion employing whatever Means prove necessary in their Judgment;"

The woodsman persisted, "Well, Socrates, what's he sayin' now?"

"If you don't want to do something—" I preempted Ed, earning a scowl. "—including paying taxes—no one will have the power to make you."

"Third, that we shall hold inviolable those Relationships among Individuals which are totally voluntary, but conversely, any Relationship not thus mutually agreeable shall be considered empty and invalid;"

"I know what that means," shouted our bucolic companion. "No more militia call-ups!"

Beside him, another rifleman asked, "But what about the Indians?"

I said, "They won't have any more militia call-ups, either."

Gallatin plowed on. "Fourth, that we shall regard Rights to be neither collective nor additive in Character—two Individuals shall have no more Rights than one, nor shall two million nor two thousand million— nor shall any Group possess Rights in excess of those belonging to its individual Members;"

The buckskinned frontiersman had a puzzled expression on his face. I opened my mouth.

"No more call-ups," said Lucy. "No matter how many folks try an' vote you into it!" She waggled her eyebrows toward a tree where a well-bandaged Cato was leaning, listening to his employer with a proud grin on his face. Lucy shrugged.

There was more: "Fifth, that we shall maintain these Principles without . . ." He returned the black man's smile. ". . . without Respect to any Person's Race, Nationality, Gender, sexual Preference, Age, or System of Beliefs, and hold that any Entity or Association, however constituted, acting to contravene them by Initiation of Force shall have forfeited its Right to exist;"

I felt a tap on my shoulder. This time I waited before I opened my mouth, and sure enough, a voice behind the rifleman said, "He says ve haf put up mit dis idiotic government und its depredations for too long, und it is time to do zomething deztructive about it!"

When the woodsman turned, he saw another bald bespectacled individual looking up at him, this one waggling his cello bow.

"My friends," said Gallatin, "I near the finish: Upon unanimous Consent of the Members or Inhabitants or any Association or Territory within the Continent of North America, we further stipulate that this Agreement shall supersede all existing governmental Documents or Usages then pertinent, that such Constitutions, Charters, Acts, Laws, Statutes, Regulations, or Ordinances contradictory or destructive to the Ends which it expresses shall be null and void, and that this Covenant, being the Property of its Authors and Signatories, shall not be subject to Interpretation excepting insofar as it shall please them."

Silence. Gallatin put the paper down, removed his glasses, and cleared his throat. "Consistent with these sentiments, I believe we must release those who may be present here against their genuine inclination. I cannot speak for anybody else; I would not. Yet to ensure their safe passage back to Pittsburgh or wherever they may wish to go, I guarantee their lives with mine." Silence turned to uproar. There were shouts, curses, a general confused babble.

"Likewise—" The noise stopped him for a moment. "Likewise, *mes enfants.*" The noise died. "Likewise, we must pledge to leave all property—save that of the excisemen, which is forfeit—unmolested. Else we become what our enemy is and lose the war by default."

Another hubbub rose at this idea, more restrained. Gallatin let it play itself out before he went on. "Our purpose has been set forth in writing. Barring emendment, I would ask each participant to sign this Covenant, make his mark before witnesses, or, without prejudice or ill-will from those who do sign, depart."

Andrew McFarlane seized the quill and laughed. "By all means, Monsoor Gallatin, spare Kirkpatrick's property. But I caution you all—say this to him when you see him—if ever he and I should meet, one of us will die!" Having warned his brother's murderer, he signed.

"So shall it be," Gallatin answered, pausing to put his own name to the document. "The suggestion has been offered by *Monsieur* Bradford that we burn Pittsburgh to the ground. *Monsieur* Brackenridge, on the other hand, would have us transform our revolution into a harmless parade. There is a third alternative, *mes amis*. Let us, indeed, proceed through Pittsburgh to demonstrate the discipline of our convictions, and to permit our numbers once again to swell—and then on to Philadelphia!"

18

Enough Rope

A Nipponese copy of a twentieth-century Filipino switchblade. A *semi*waterproof fuse that managed to get lit in an eighteenth-century downpour, likely with a twenty-first-century laser. One anachronism calls for another.

That's how a tired twenty-second century detective came to be among the signatories to Gallatin's "New Covenant," scheduled, in another year or so, to become the backbone of the Revised Articles of Confederation—replacing the Federalist Party's hated Constitution.

It's a matter of recorded fact.

Ed, a Confederate native and boyhood social studies victim, had always assumed it was just some unrelated namesake, this "Edward William Bear" who'd put his name to the revolutionary document in 1794. Not having grown up in the Confederacy—and being more interested in the Declaration of Independence (containing Gallatin's "one little word," tragically missing in my world)—I never noticed the "coincidence."

Taking the quill, I signed for both of us. Lucy signed with disappearing ink, supplied by Ooloorie, and passed the pen to Ochskahrt. In our century, their names would still be visible, when sprayed with just the right mixture of turpentine, sour milk, and parrot guano. As others crowded in to add their marks, word filtered back to the camp. Soon a line of would-be John Hancocks stretched through the woods, across the tent-covered field. Gallatin called for a monkathon—more parchment, ink, relays of individuals with decent penmanship—to copy out the Covenant so it would appear in full on every page.

The quill, at last, came to Brackenridge.

The Pittsburgh mouthpiece leaned over the improvised table, sweat beading his forehead. Pen in hand, he turned to the crowd. "Y-yes, by all means . . . although I confess it's a simple march I still advocate—with no other view than to give proof to the Executive that the strictest order can be preserved among us and no damage done."

Boos and hisses, unimpeded by any notion of civility a later era might have demanded. The professional mugwump didn't hear, kept on talking, inwardly directed. "That's it, we'll march through the town and, taking a turn, come out again upon the plain of the Monongahela, and, sampling some whiskey with the inhabitants—you boys all relish whiskey—embark across the river."

Gallatin placed a hand over Brackenridge's, removed the pen. "You are under no obligation, *Monsieur*."

Benjamin Parkinson seized the lawyer's lapels, his freckled face flushing with an anger that leaked out between clenched teeth. "It is well for you that Mr. Gallatin has resolved matters in Christian charity. Elsewise, you would have been taken notice of, you... *gentlemen.* If we go to Pittsburgh, sir, we won't be going for whiskey!"

Brackenridge's hands fluttered like frightened birds. "B-but I meant no more than that we should *drink* together, and not any offense whatever! Mr. Parkinson, it would affect me in a sensible manner if anything inadvertently said by me should interrupt harmony and injure the cause."

A frozen moment.

Parkinson threw his head back, roaring with laughter. It began to echo all around until Brackenridge, face as red as Parkinson's had been, slouched off to the margin of the clearing.

"*Huzza for Tom the Tinker!*" Beside me, a scruffy rifleman put his wear-stained hat over the pitted muzzle of his weapon. Twirling it aloft, he shouted, "Onward to wealthy Sodom! I've a bad hat now, but'll have a better one soon!"

Gallatin trod through the crowd, seized the rifle, threw it to the ground. "For shame! It is not we who are thieves, but the collectors. Sign the Covenant, swear yourself to its provisions, or by the good God, be gone!" It was the first I'd ever seen him angry. As surprised reaction to his uncharacteristic tirade rippled through the crowd, I noticed that Brackenridge had disappeared.

"Trying to round up members of the Pittsburgh

bunch." Ed was in touch with the encyclopedia in his head again. "I'm going to follow him!"

"The hell you are," I said. "Watch Gallatin. Tell Lucy." I was gone before he had a chance to protest. Soon I was through the trees, out of eyeshot of the clearing. Glancing around, I stopped to take my clothes off. I hadn't had much opportunity to experiment with my skinsuit, but familiar with its predecessors, I played with the inset buttons. Patterns chased each other across the surface, plaids and polka-dots and paisleys. With some finagling, the light-sensitive layers began picking up whatever was behind me—trees and bushes—transmitting it to the front. Meanwhile, the front relayed what it saw to my back. Not perfect, but for optical purposes, I became a part of the woods I moved through. Invisible.

Camouflaging myself as whatever Arbor Day centerpiece I happened to be standing near at the moment, I stopped, disguised as a clump of lilacs near the edge of the tent-cluttered field. Further north and east stood a whitewashed frame farmhouse where the Committee was meeting.

I lay outside, just under a glass-paned window, pretending to be the annex to a blackened tree stump. Laying a fingertip on the sill as a periscope, I stepped up my senses. The inner surface of my hood filled with an indoor scene. My suit-augmented hearing was nothing short of phenomenal—and what I could learn of my surroundings from just a casual sniff would have filled encyclopedias. I reduced the audio of my suit-receptors, stopped down the—what, smellio?—as far as it would go. Just didn't have the olfactory lobes to tolerate it.

Hugh Henry was inside, sending men to find the rest of the Committee. The impromptu meeting would be assembled from whatever Pittsburghers could be rounded up. Brackenridge was in something transcending even his usual funk, insisting an altogether new course of action be outlined to deal with Gallatin's philosophical bombshell. *Fast*.

Paradoxically convinced the rebels were uncivilizable animals—and at the same time harbored a Presbyterian resentment against the fleshpots of Pittsburgh—members were appointed to collect whiskey, bring it to the plain east of town to "refresh" the troops. Every store and tavern was to be ordered closed—no liquor to be *sold* to the rebels. Meanwhile, individual townsmen would be encouraged to contribute from their provisions. That way, there'd be no excuse for the rebels breaking ranks and wandering about through the city streets.

"The insurrectionists are in an *ugly* mood," Brackenridge maintained. "There is no doubt in my mind that they plan to plunder the town. I have it on the best authority that numbers of rebel women on Coal Hill are waiting to see its destruction, and to help their men accomplish it."

John Wilkins, Sr., asked, "And what authority is that, Hugh Henry?"

"Why, er . . . never mind, sir! Little Edna—" The lawyer stopped. "—that is, my informant assures me it is so."

I grinned to myself. Coal Hill housed, among its

other distinctions, the closest thing Pittsburgh could claim to a red-light district. Brief, embarrassed silence. Mention of his informant, however, erased my grin as it formed. First a common woods-runner, then a mail-carrier, now Edna was masquerading as vice-squad bait. Manipulating arm-buttons, I tried to get in touch with Ed or Lucy, but before I could, the farmhouse conversation picked up again.

"Very well," said minimagnate Wilkins. "If so, let it be individual householders the burden falls on, not the interests represented here." There was a buzz of cynical assent. More important, they decided neither to sign Gallatin's seditious, anarchistic Covenant (not much chance of that anyway, and the actual words were "republican" and "Jacobin"), nor permit its circulation in town. Who was it said "I don't care who does the voting as long as I do the nominating"?

A number of the Committee, alarmed and nervous at the prospect of invasion, excused themselves, setting out for town to hide whatever papers and valuables they hadn't already concealed. They invited Hugh Henry to ride along. He assured them he'd sent orders to have his own closet-skeletons ferried across the river to the home of a friend, and volunteered to continue risking life and limb to keep a responsible eye on the rebel camp.

Some wag, better informed than the rest, mentioned the irresistible favors of Coal Hill's "*kleine* Edna Klute, the Pennsylvania Dutch treat." *Ahem! Snort! Fap!* After a humiliated Brackenridge, lawyer and well-known family-man, finished with his Major Hoople act, he shooed the others out, locked the door, and waddled toward the sleeping quarters at the back of the house.

Where someone was waiting—a familiar someone. She was putting out a cigarette in a pewter saucer when I managed to sneak around the corner, into place below the appropriate window. A pile of tea-crates made a fair hunting blind. "Mine liebchen Hugh Henry!" she growled in a sultry voice filtered through a phony accent. "Are you t'rough at lazt mit doze boring men, dollink?"

"Er, um, ahem . . . " Brackenridge was momentarily deprived of eloquence. Edna reclined on the crazy-quilt of a large brass bed, traveling cloak and other clothing tossed on a nearby chair. The damage to her skinsuit must have been fatal. In its place, she wore black pantyhose, leg-warmers, topped with a red- and black-striped leotard. It was having a visible effect on the fit at Hugh Henry's inseam.

"Come, mine treasure-box," she said without waiting for an answer, "zit bezide me und your meeting tell me all about. You know how I take an interest in politics."

The lawyer complied, leaving jacket, shoes, waistcoat, and knee-britches trailed on the floor behind him. Men's underwear any century looks ridiculous. His was no exception. As she preened him, he summarized events, answering an occasional question. She worked him like one of Dr. Skinner's rats, rewarding responses, subtly withholding the reward when there was more she wanted. "Exzellent, dumplingkeit, with our plans it all works out. Listen, now, while Edna tells you what must be done." It was clear there were other things he'd rather have attended to, but he listened. "I have told you I am from the future—a future that must not be allowed to come to pass. We must change events here and now so that another future is created. Have you understood this?"

"Well, yes..." answered Brackenridge. "After a fashion."

"Very well, after a fashion you may understand that, in this future from which I come, a great deal of technological progress has been made—'mechanical,' if you do not understand that other word. We can do things that cannot be done in your day and age. Understanden zee?"

"No."

"It matters not. Once we have this Gallatin and his friends from my century out of the way, I can use what I know to direct the course of events. In some universes, a second war will be fought with England. In the universe we create together, England will lose. Canada will be absorbed into the United States, and, within a century, this country will become the center of a world empire that takes in the entire known galaxy—with me as its Empress. Am I going too fast for you?"

"Not fast enough, my darling," replied a frustrated Brackenridge, "but you will always be the Empress of my heart."

"How nice." Her accent was gone now, but the fat attorney didn't seem to notice. "What we must do is crush this rebellion before it gets underway. Do you think you can do that for me?" He nodded, and she took this as her cue to reward him, directing his head where it would do her the most good. Running one hand through his hair, she lit another cigarette, enjoying two vices at the same time. "Very good," she said to the unhearing Brackenridge. "Faster, if you please."

Gentle reader, there arrives a moment when a discreet curtain must be drawn over ensuing events—in order to keep from throwing up. I never thought sex was a spectator sport, and with that pair, I'd rather have watched a good horror movie. When it was over, they started putting on their clothes, preparing to leave by separate ways, Brackenridge to Braddock's Field, Edna back to Coal Hill.

One of the tea-crates splintered, dropping me six inches. Inside, Edna froze, whirled to face the window, metal in her hand. Surprised, I threw my arms up. Energy splashed. Blackness. I wasn't unconscious. I think it was my suit's way of dealing with the overload a laser represented. When I got the hood peeled down, the exterior was mirror-silver. Pistol in hand, I peeked back through the window. The room was empty.

So was the house.

I wasn't inclined to confer with anyone until I'd thought it through. Edna might be taken care of on the Coal Hill road—dispatch one of us to dispatch her. But playing bodyguard and playing detective are two different—and mutually exclusive—games. The first calls for sticking to the client, the second for just the opposite. I kept coming back to the same damned conclusions: there weren't enough of us, even for adequate guard-duty; we couldn't recruit even the friendliest locals, they wouldn't be prepared to deal with paratronic reconnaissance and energy weapons, let alone the fact that we existed; the idea was to keep Gallatin alive, not play cops and dopers; Edna had a way of slipping through your fingers—knowing she'd been seen here, there was no guarantee she'd head back to Coal Hill; but—good news, I think—eventually she'd come to us.

By the time I staggered back to the clearing, I'd shared these observations with the others. Seated around the rough-plank table where Covenant signers still trickled through, Gallatin conferred with the other leaders. The Committee of Twenty-one had gone home. Now he proposed to send Bradford, along with half a dozen friends of Fort Fayette's commandant, to assure the old boy that our troops were on the way—but with no intention of disturbing the fort.

"I would have you request," he told the overdressed state's attorney, "that they permit us to march by. The Fort is for protection against Indians. We have no business with it."

Despite his fervor, even Bradford was reluctant to precipitate conflict. "There's a deal of powder and shot inside, from use of which we might benefit. We could take the fort, with casualties, but not without risking their destruction."

Gallatin agreed. "It is my desire to prevent any incident that might fulfill *Monsieur* Brackenridge's low opinion of us."

"Brackenridge didn't go back with the Committee," I spoke up. "I think he's somewhere in camp."

He nodded again. "Then we shall ask him to go along. He will be hoping for the worst to happen. You will go, *Monsieur* Bear, to ensure that it does not?"

I looked to Ed and Lucy. He shrugged, and she raised her first in a radical salute. Ten minutes later, I was doing Gene Autry imitations.

In one of those fortunate accidents of history, almost an afterthought, Bradford brought a copy of the Covenant. Fort Fayette was in better condition than Couch's Fort, but of the same raised earth and palisade. The gate was open. Men wearing random parts of uniforms lounged about.

Coming to the gate, Butler invited us inside, listened, scanned the document. He was a stout, red-faced man, with round shiny cheeks and steel-wool-colored muttonchops below his white wig. Retaining the parchment, he asked to be excused for half an hour to think. We visitors sat in the dirt-floored yard, surrounded by soldiers, fearing any moment we might be arrested. It was a long half hour.

Butler returned, in full dress uniform. "Mr. Brackenridge, I am surprised. Are you with these traitorous dogs?" I thought, there goes the ball-game. My rifle was beside me, but other eyes were on it. I laid a hand on my knife.

Glancing from one of his rebel companions to another—with a look reserved between for the Major's enormous sword in its polished scabbard—the lawyer sweated. "No, sir, I represent responsible interests whose desire is to limit their seditious and destructive tendencies."

He stepped across the yard to seek refuge at the Major's side.

"You turncoat!" Bradford leaped to his feet. "You

Benedict! You Judas! You would betray your own mother to the side that could benefit you most!"

"I believe I agree with you, Mr. Prosecutor," said Butler. Pointing first at Brackenridge, then toward a log-end jutting high from the compound wall, he commanded, "Hang me that dog!"

19

Roll Out the Barrel

Brackenridge stood, paralyzed speechless as a pair of ragged bluecoats handed muskets to their comrades, moved to either side of him, and seized his arms. In nominal charge of the expedition, Bradford lunged forward, stopped, then turned to look at me. "If some of you men will help them," he shrugged, "the deed should have been done ere long ago."

Two rebels rose to comply. At a corner of the fort, where a watchtower sat atop the wall, one of the logs had been left three feet longer than the rest. A deep groove was worn across its top. A soldier threw a length of hemp over it, flipping at the rope until it settled in the groove. He made an end fast to a brass cleat that would have looked more at home on the gunwale of a flatboat. The other end he fashioned into a noose. A heavy whiskey keg was rolled out of a storage lean-to, set under the jutting log-end.

Brackenridge's wrists had been forced behind his

rotund body, bound with a thong. He'd found his voice, and opened up to protest. Bradford seized the opportunity to whip a lace-edged handkerchief from his sleeve and thrust it into the lawyer's mouth. He turned to me. "You know, I've wanted to do that since I was a boy."

Leaving heel-ruts in the dirt behind them, an escort of four, two soldiers, two rebels, frog-marched Brackenridge toward the upended keg. Overhead, the noose swung in the still air. Wondering what to do—or whether I should do anything—I laughed, then put a hand on Butler's shoulder, whispering in his hairy ear. He nodded. "*Hold*!" cried the major, striding across the yard. With a middle-aged grunt, he bent and tipped the keg on its side.

Brackenridge refused to step up on the liquor barrel. I had my own doubts whether it would support him. At the major's order, the soldiers drew spike bayonets from their belt-hangers, fixed them to their muskets, upended the weapons, began stabbing the soil millimeters from the lawyer's toes. Still he refused to budge. Frustrated, Butler drew his pistol, levering back the flint. "Now climb up, sir! Climb up or I shall shoot you where you stand!"

Shoulders drooping, Brackenridge climbed up on the keg. It rocked, end-to-end, threatening to roll out from under him. The noose was slipped around his neck. The slack was taken up.

"A capital idea, Mr. Bear!" said Bradford. He shouted across the yard. "Counselor, you're a man who believes in moderation and balance, you've told me so a thousand times. See if you can balance there awhile." The men laughed, soldiers and rebels alike.

The lawyer's eyes showed white around the irises above the kerchief sticking out of his mouth. He twisted and dodged, trying to stay atop the keg.

"That," announced Major Thomas Butler, indicating Brackenridge with a back-tossed thumb, "was my last act as a Federalist." The Pittsburgher almost lost it then, feet rolling out from under him. A groan escaped through the yardgoods. He hopped and jerked, somehow bringing the barrel to rest again under his heels.

Ignoring the life-and-death struggle behind him, the commandant unfurled a familiar roll of parchment, seized me by a shoulder, and turned me around. I felt him scrawl something, using my back for a clipboard. "That," announced Citizen Thomas Butler, "constitutes my first act as a Gallatinist!"

He handed the paper to Bradford, becoming, in that moment, the first to employ a political label which, over the next two centuries, would sweep the world clean of established authority. To his second-in-command, he delivered the resignation he'd written during his half hour of meditation. At the gate, he paused, drew his officer's-issue wrist-breaker from its steel scabbard. With a grunt, he snapped the blade over one knee, threw the pieces to one side. "Mr. Bradford, I would request permission to enlist at once, as a private soldier, in Mr. Gallatin's Army of Rebellion. Can this be accomplished?"

Bradford looked down at the parchment, as if it had turned out to be a treasure-map. He looked back at the major. "It can, sir, and it has!"

Behind them, there was a cheer. The top edge of the wall was lined with soldiers, waving their hats. A few discharged their muskets into the air. We rebels, with our VIP recruit, waved back and began to mount our horses as Butler's men, his former command, continued watching. There was an excited shout: "Stay a moment, sir. We beg you, stay!"

The row of heads disappeared from the serried wall-top. Where we stood, we could hear a buzz of conversation, some of it pretty loud. Then another cheer. Then silence. Within five minutes the entire structure had emptied itself of humanity, some six or seven Federalists dissenters hitching their muskets over their blue-coated shoulders and dispersing into the countryside. The rest, eighteen or nineteen in all, came through the gate, queued up to sign the Covenant below the name of their former commander, and surrendered the fort to Bradford in the name of Gallatin. Our strength now tripled, those with horses saddled up and began the march along Braddock's Field Road to join the main body of rebels.

Even counting those who'd accepted the Swiss philosopher's guarantee and decamped, that body would be thousands strong. The addition we'd accomplished wasn't impressive in terms of numbers, yet we knew—whether we were living through it for the first time like Butler and Bradford, or had read about it in history books—that Gallatin had won his first real victory.

And Brackenridge? For all I know he's still there, the solitary occupant of Fort Fayette, teetering on his whiskey keg.

I rode toward the rear of the column, risking a moment's communion with my suit to catch up on events. The disguise I'd programmed onto the hood happened to be my own face, complete with an authentically dumb expression.

"That's good news," Ed enthused by, *"though we knew, of course, that that's what was going to happen."*

Ignoring the debate between determinism and free will that kicked off in my head, I watched Lucy shake hers—through her husband's eyes. *"I ain't too sanguine about that whiskey-barrel bit, Winnie."* Within the privacy of my hood, I grinned. She was under a strain, torn between the ethics of time-travel and the fact that she thought what had happened was funny. *"I don't remember nothin' about no hangin'."*

Ed laughed. *"If Win's destroyed the universe, it was worth it! I wish I could have been there!"*

"Stand by for transmission, then," I said. "I recorded everything." I keyed the information-transfer. While they watched the necktie party, I sneaked a look at my real surroundings. The column plodded on as before. My short-subject received rave reviews. I'd never known they had a taste for snuff-films. Probably the arty way I'd left things hanging at the end.

In Braddock's Field, fife and drum bleating and beating, the anti-tax militia had begun its eight-mile march to Pittsburgh. In good order, for a bunch of anarchists. Arrayed in a line stretching two and a half miles, armed and dangerous men took their places. Before Gallatin, they'd merely been armed. We were supposed to catch up where Braddock's Field Road intersected Fourth Street, joining the march through the rest of the city, back to the Monongahela—where all available marine transport was being collected by a Committee we had no reason to trust—over the river, and on to Philadelphia. If we were late, we'd miss the boat.

"There've been more politics, however," Ed warned. He was riding alongside Lucy and Ochskahrt, enjoying the excursion.

"Oh?" I peeked out to make sure I wasn't being observed by my own companions.

"Yes, the conscientious nonsigners—a minority numbering well into the hundreds—have announced, for various reasons, an intention to remain neutral in the coming struggle—"

Lucy, indignant, interrupted: "There's even a minority *of* the minority, Winnie, Federalists, threatenin' to oppose the Rebellion—"

"After a decent interval," Ed finished for her. "In all truth, their parting with the rest of us was more than cordial."

I shook my head. "Like the last day at West Point, just before the Civil War. Beginning things like gentlemen didn't make it a single drop less bloody."

"Gallatin's promised them safe-passage," Ed persisted, "and they've dispersed."

"Lotsa luck to 'em," Lucy sneered. "None of it good!"

The day wore on. We were late hooking up with the rest, but not fatally, catching up in the middle of Pittsburgh on Market Street. We weren't much to look at. About a third of what Butler had called "Gallatin's Army" were mounted—we'd never claimed to be the *Cavalry* of Rebellion. Fewer than that had guns, and a healthy percentage weren't even wearing shoes. They'd have to follow Napoleon's advice (still a few more years in the future) and march on their stomachs. Perennial chairman-of-everything Edward Cook, along with David Hamilton, had been appointed overall commanders, Gabriel Blakeney officer of day. Sounded to me like the work of some committee. Gallatin rode up and down the line pleading with the men not to call him "General." Andrew McFarlane took the point— pardon me, "commanded the advance guard." He still had blood in his eye and wanted to be first to spot Kirkpatrick. No one could talk him out of it.

But we didn't see Kirkpatrick. It was one of those good-news/bad-news things. When the column clip-clopped into Pittsburgh, its commanders, officer of the day, advance guard, and reluctant generalissimo were provided with graphic evidence of genuine urban sentiment. Between late morning and mid-afternoon, the people had risen against the Committee and taken back their town. They hadn't been as charitable as Thomas Butler—Market Street was lined with the bodies of Committee members, swinging from their broken necks. As we rode through, and off on the long trail to the capital, the repeated cry was "On to Philadelphia— that's where they said they wanted us! Now they shall have us there!"

Gallatin had more problems. At the last minute, just before the first relay of boats was launched, he learned of a plot to fire the town houses of the Nevilles, Edward Day, John Gibson, and James Brison. Headquartered in Wilkins' General Store, Gallatin handled it well. He had the conspirators in for a chat, and that was that.

No fire, at least not then. A Captain Maximillian Riddle, however, elected leader of the yellow hunting-shirted "Riddle's Raiders," considered the most "active" of the insurgents, set fire to Kirkpatrick's town house at 9 P.M. It wasn't the only incident of its kind. Word came that a revenue collector named Reagan had been tarred and feathered in Westmoreland County. The house of his colleague-in-crime, Benjamin Wells, had been burned to the ground. Collector John Webster was attacked in Bedford County.

By dawn, Gallatin had a couple of other items on his hands. The men had stopped with "General" and had begun calling him "Mr. President." Also, Andrew McFarlane couldn't be found anywhere. He caught up as the last of us climbed out of our boats on the other side of the river, covered with sweat and soot and smelling of whale oil. The last we saw of Pittsburgh was a column of smoke from the burning of Kirkpatrick's barn across the river.

20

Let George Do It

MORRIS HOUSE, PHILADELPHIA, PA.
SUNDAY, AUGUST 3, 1794

DRAMATIS   GEORGE WASHINGTON,
PERSONAE: PRESIDENT OF THE UNITED STATES
             ALEXANDER HAMILTON,
               SECRETARY OF THE TREASURY
             THOMAS MIFFLIN,
               GOVERNOR OF PENNSYLVANIA
             UNITED STATES ATTORNEY
               GENERAL *WILLIAM* BRADFORD
             ALEXANDER JAMES
               DALLAS, SECRETARY OF THE
                 COMMONWEALTH
             PENNSYLVANIA CHIEF
               JUSTICE THOMAS McKEAN

WASHINGTON: "Friends, I wish to open this meeting by call-
             ing attention to the gravity of the present
             crisis. We in the east watch developments
             in the Monongahela country with increasing

175

anxiety. I must assert that the most spirited and firm measures are necessary to prevent the overthrow of the Constitution and of the Laws."

HAMILTON: "My dear friends, let there be no illusion within the official circles as to the importance of this crisis. What lovelier, what more defensible opportunity could be presented, in the attempt to build the power and prestige of our government, than this heaven-sent rebellion in the west? If we are to survive, the democrats must be scotched. As for effective scotching, we are offered an enforcement of the funding system."

WASHINGTON: "Quite so. You well express my determination to go to every length the Constitution and Laws will permit. For the present, no further. But here: the actions of the general government will necessarily be slow, since it must wait for certification that the disorders are beyond control by judicial authority. I inquire if there is not some way the Commonwealth could cooperate by adopting preliminary measures."

MIFFLIN: (Uncomfortably) "Sir, I am reminded ... of the prophecy that the federal government would ultimately swallow up the states. I cannot help interpreting this proposal as a step in that direction."

BRADFORD: "See here, Mifflin, this is nonsense! We are all aware, are we not, of the law of 1783 which authorizes the governor of this commonwealth to call out the militia in sudden emergencies?"

DALLAS: "Ha. And I would point out to you, Mr. Bradford, that this law, in which you seek such grateful refuge, was in its tenure much overused, and has long since been repealed!"
(Turning to the president) "In answer to Mr. Bradford's questioning, Your Excellency, I am compelled to tender it as my earnest opinion that our governor, precisely like yourself, is obliged to await upon a judicial certificate before he can be authorized to call out the militia. I am sorry, sir, but there it is."

WASHINGTON: (Irritated) "But there it shall not long remain, Mr. Dallas. I wish to make clear my intention to proceed against the rioters by military means."

McKEAN: "And I, sir, wish to assure you in the most unequivocal of terms possible that the judiciary power is more than equal to the task of quelling and punishing these riots. The overhasty employment of military force, at this period, would be as bad as anything the rioters have done—as well as being equally unconstitutional and illegal."

HAMILTON: "A pox on constitutionality! I'll not waste time rehearsing the celebrated causes of western discontent. They are endless, nor will they vanish overnight. Like faithless lovers, they have slighted our caresses, and for that reason, I agree with our President, insisting that the crisis be met by an immediate resort to arms!"

DALLAS: (Spreading his hands) "I would comment only that in the opinion of Judge Alexander Addison of Pittsburgh, force will promote resistance to what inevitably must be taken as an attempt to dragoon the people into submission."

HAMILTON: "Addison? Why, that horrible man is himself one of the most insidious promoters of opposition! Do not look at me that way! My draft report to our President contains many particulars of Judge Addison's seditious conduct."

I'll bet you're wondering how the hell we got hold of *that* recording. Father of his Country, and so on. It's a long story. I'll get around to it—within limits of plausible deniability.

Washington had called the meeting at his residence on *Philadelphia*'s Market Street just before news of the previous day's rebel march through Pittsburgh had reached the capital. Besides the President, most of the bigwigs from the federal government and Pennsylvania were present, including those who did all that talking, plus Secretary of State Edmund Randolph and Secretary of War Harry Knox. In addition to the governor, chief justice, and state secretary representing the Keystone State, its Attorney General, Jared Ingersoll, sat in.

And never said a word.

A paratronic conference with Ooloorie had resulted in the decision, disagreeable to all, that, now the Rebellion was well underway, one of us ought to shift attention to the other end and keep tabs on what the badguys were up to. The local badguys. Lucy and Ed had ransacked Coal Hill without finding a trace of Edna. I suspected one of them jiggered the straws, but couldn't prove it. At that, it saved me the long march with the troops.

So it began with another unforgettable Pittsburgh evening. The night was dark and the moon was yellow—I'm not even going to consider what came tumbling down, on account of the location. I was against it, but there was only one way a stranger in that crowd could get any privacy.

In the shadowy darkness, a wary hand on the butt of the pistol I'd swapped Ed the rifle for, I stumbled through an alley cluttered with what would someday be expensive antiques—right now, they were just somebody's garbage—trying to find the tiny shack I'd called my own a few days before. The alley didn't look at all the same at night. Nothing seemed familiar. The galvanized steel garbage can hadn't been invented, nor the telephone pole, nor the automobile from which abandoned hulks and piles of threadbare tires are fashioned. In short, the typical American alley hadn't yet been elevated to the art-form it would later become.

I was lost. Either side of me, beyond buttoned-up houses and storefronts, bedlam reigned as a townlet of one thousand tried to find room for five times that number. True, the strangers had brought their own tents and bedrolls. It was surface-area to stretch them out on that presented a problem. In a one-horse town, even sleeping in the manger was out.

Somewhere a tomcat yodeled the Indian love-call. I took a whiff. The cool of the evening had subdued its homey aroma a trifle, but there it was, the rustic phone booth where I'd earlier conferred with Ooloorie.

I crept up, wary that some desperate soul might have hit on it as a place to sleep.

Empty. I latched the crescent-pierced door behind me, reflecting that, without the flies, it just wasn't the same place. I keyed my sleeve-buttons. "Kirk to *Enterprise*, beam me up."

A point of hellish blue hung in the darkness. *"Landling, you will make bad jokes upon your deathbed."* The point dilated, staying painful to look at on the edges. I stepped through into San Francisco of the twenty-second century, and the Emperor Norton University.

Surrounding me on every side was complicated machinery, humming with pent-up power. All four walls of the white-tiled room were transparent, one a breathtaking cityscape—the Golden Gate had never been constructed here, but the broad, hovercraft-carpeted sea-lane taking its place was still filled with spume-spraying fireflies, preserved, like the cable-cars, as part of the historic atmosphere.

The other three transparencies—and, heaven help me, the ceiling—sloshed with salty water in which swam an equally salty silver-gray figure, armless, legless, half again as long as a man, with twice the advertised intelligence (compared to mine, at least) and a quarter of the sense of humor.

I was in an *air* tank, from her point of view. "Greetings, oceanling, get any herring pickled lately?"

The porpoise thrashed her tail. "There is nothing to be gained from surrealistic conversation, Edward William Bear. We have succeeded in determining arrival coordinates for eighteenth-century Philadelphia. I am feeding the values to the machinery by direct-wired mind-link to assure their accuracy." Not belonging to a species with fingers, Ooloorie distrusted all machinery and its operators. She seldom left her clammy cloister for any reason—although a skinsuit would have made it easy—preferring the cerebral pursuit of science and mathematics.

A hissing, rustling noise caught my attention. I turned toward an empty corner of the room. Through the otherwise solid-looking floor, like toothpaste, rose a small stack of twenty-first-century information chips. "You cannot appear in ancient Philadelphia without advance intelligence," Ooloorie told me. "Since you have no implant, we shall feed these data into your suit."

I nodded, reluctant to rush affairs. This room was a nice place to be, compared to what I'd just left—or to the whole eighteenth century, for that matter. "Swell. When do I go back?"

"In approximately five minutes. We are new at this time-travel business. Insufficient calibratory accuracy. Otherwise, I would let you get a good night's sleep and send you back to the minute you left Pittsburgh. Give me another decade, I shall be capable of such feats."

"But Ooloorie, dear," I objected, inserting the information chips through a slot in my sleeve, "you haven't *got* any feets."

She roiled the water with her tail. "You try my patience, human. I have no obligation to tolerate such nonsense." With an annoyed lash, the cetacean swam deeper into the misty distance.

"What's wrong with you, a case of barnacles?" I'd

known the scientist more than a century. She'd never been the life of the party. "Or are you sore because you didn't invent time-travel before Hirnschlag?"

There was a long, silent pause, then she said, "Worse, landling, at least from where I stand."

"Swim," I corrected, then regretted it. "Sorry."

"Forgiven, Win—it is also the point that rankles me. That, and what you said about 'feets.' It is my daughter, Leelalee, do you know her?"

I recalled a long-ago letter from one of my own girls—maybe it was Koko Featherstone-Haugh—from the *Tom Paine Maru*. "A starship captain or something like that?"

"Something like that. She has spent the last several decades working among humans and simians. Now she has decided to help colonize a sea-planet recently discovered."

"That's bad, is it?"

"Leelalee has decided that she needs to grow a pair of hands."

"Hmmmm." I blinked. "Didn't know they could do that. Still..."

Across the room, adjustments began making themselves on the Broach machinery. I hated to see that. I was enjoying a microvacation in a century I understood. Ooloorie went on, "Genetic manipulation of somatic tissue. How would you feel if your daughters decided to join a religious cult. Or become Hamiltonians. Or grew a set of moose-antlers. Do not laugh— that is how it seems to me, Win. A porpoise needs a pair of hands—"

"Like a fish needs a bicycle," I finished.

"Manipulatory organs are for less-gifted intelligences. Those better off should appreciate the pure cognition it affords them."

I was used to Ooloorie's offhand insults. That's just the way she was. Now I heard bitterness in her tone. Professor Deejay Thorens had been like a daughter to the porpoise—yet she, too, had emigrated. Had it been to avoid being considered second-class offspring? I opened my mouth, but considering the lame excuse for commiseration I was about to offer, it was a good thing the scientist interrupted before I got started.

"I have reshipped the primary moebius coil, Edward William Bear. I am sorry that this apparatus is so clumsy. What Edna Janof did to Hirnschlag von Ochskahrt's equipment left little available for reuse."

"Just so long as it doesn't dump me out in hyperspace—" I tapped the pistol in my belt. "—or back somewhere with the dinosaurs."

"I've one more thing to show you." Through the floor rose a naked scalp, followed by a red-rimmed pair of the angriest eyes I've ever seen. Below was a gag, and below that, as it rose to our level, a body in eighteenth-century clothing—except for the handcuffs, belly-chains, and leg-irons. If I'd learned my history right, it was none other than Pennsylvania State Attorney General Jared Ingersoll.

"Obscenity!" cried Ooloorie. "The stasis-field has worn off—it was set for ten hours!"

I walked over to the prisoner. He glared up at me as I spoke. "My sympathies, buddy, I know how it feels to be Broach-napped." Turning to Ooloorie, I asked, "What are you going to do with him now?"

The dolphin shuddered, "Misplace him somewhere, I suppose—the paradoxes..."

I shook my head. "Keep him on ice until this operation's over. I've seen enough killing for a lifetime. Promise?"

"Landling, I cannot. We may need to appropriate more Hamiltonians to provide you with disguises. My mind has been preoccupied. All I can promise is to be more careful henceforward."

The conversation didn't interest Ingersoll. He strained against his bonds as I stepped toward the Broach aperture. The last I saw of him, as I instructed my suit to imitate his face, were those fear-maddened eyes.

21

The Times That
Try Men's Soles

AUGUST 23, 1794

Civilization's in the eye of the beholder.

The City of Botherly Love looked like Pittsburgh to me, piled higher and deeper. What did I know? This cluster of antique colonial architecture was thirty times the size of the smaller, western town, was, in fact, the largest in the country. It had more streets, and more of them were cobbled. It had more houses, shops, horses, people ...

One of them stopped me now and asked me for the time. I looked like I had it, in my Respectable Businessman disguise. Jared Ingersoll I'd sloughed on leaving Morris House. I faked extracting a pocket-watch I didn't own, keeping my elbow close to my body. The ornate timepiece and chain were "painted" on, a decorative feature my suit was generating. The inside of the same suit told me what time it was. The tall dark gentleman nodded and went on his way.

And . . . what had I been thinking about? Oh yeah—but not one traffic light did Philadelphia possess, nor fire hydrant, taco-stand or hamburger joint. No movie theaters, gay bars, or speedy car washes. And just *try* getting your nickel back from a pay phone.

The guy never suspected he was being tailed.

I gave the Secretary a block's lead. I had a good idea where he was going, a big house in a neighborhood that had seen nobler times. He owned the place through a tangle of business connections. This was the fellow, after all, who'd invented Chase Manhattan. He went inside; I gave him a few minutes. I needed the time, too. At five foot seven and two hundred ten, shinnying drain pipes isn't my idea of fun. Nobody in the carriage just pulling up would notice an irregular lump of brick jutting from the third floor of a run-down private residence.

Two minutes passed. Through the bedroom window, I watched Edna enter, throw off her cloak, hollering something toward a room next door. Behind a decorative screen, she began unfastening fastenings, flopping garments over the top. Underneath, she wore that same striped outfit with the leg-warmers, but it wouldn't be like Braddock's Field, this time. When I had a clear shot, I was going to cool Edna for good.

From the next room, Hamilton emerged—and almost cost me my grip. He was dressed the way I'd first seen Lucy, back at Gary's Bait & Trust: Merry Widow, black mesh stockings, button earrings, feather boa. "Ah, my little Edna," he gushed. "You should not have taken advantage of my sensibilities to steal into my affections without consent."

She wrinkled her nose. "What?"

"But," he went on, "as we are generally indulgent to those we love, I shall not scruple to pardon the fraud you have committed. Hasten to give us pleasure which we shall relish." He spread his arms, advancing a step. She backed up one. "But mind you, *a la française*, not *a l'americaine*." She retreated another pace, only to be blocked by a bureau. He seized her, clasped her to his bosom.

"Cold in my professions," he nuzzled her, smearing makeup on her shoulder, "warm in friendships, I wish, by action rather than words, to convince you. I had another friend, once, a clever fellow. We knew each other's sentiments, our views were the same. Alas, all men love egotism—*adieu,* God bless him—he'd more of the infirmities of human nature than others. We fought side by side to make America free. He could not quit his sword and struggle, hand in hand, to make her happy."

Struggling herself, for breathing-space, Edna wedged an arm between them. "I think I understand." She nodded. She reached back to the bureau. There was a *crack!* as she brandished the carriage whip she'd laid there. "You're a bad boy, Alex; you'll have to be punished!"

Hamilton threw himself to his knees, palms together in supplication. "You have disarmed my discontent, my dear, and by a single mark of attention made up the quarrel!" Tears of joy streamed down his face as he sobbed, "Your impatience is well placed. I confess my sins; my affection was alarmed, and my vanity piqued. Mistress, let friendship between us be more than a name. Be witness to the final consummation!"

I'm broad-minded, but what they did then, I hadn't even known was anatomically possible. I'm ashamed to admit that I forgot all about assassinating Edna. And I'll never be able to look at a buttonhook again. When it was over, and they were getting dressed, I rested my flintlock on the upper casement, aligned the sights with Edna's torso—

"Say, you, what are you doing, there?"

"GHAAA!" I let go of the casement, almost dropped the pistol, grabbed for the drain pipe. Bits of mortar crumbled into the alley below, where a man looked up, armed with a double-barreled shotgun. They heard him inside, too. I turned in time to see Edna fumbling through her clothing for her gun. Hamilton cowered in a corner, trying to cover his corset with his hands.

I fired. Smoke and flame spat through the shattered window. The ball—not the disintegrating type— smashed an oil lamp inches from the Secretary's nose. He shrieked, "The rebels!" threw both arms in the air, and made a Hamilton-shaped hole in the bedroom door. No spare hand to cock the pistol with. Edna leveled her plasma piece at me. I dropped the flintlock, slapped buttons, stepped off the edge, my suit rigid as steel. I landed on the shotgunner, waited for my suit to relax, grabbed my pistol, and sprayed the window above with Heller radiation.

Hamilton ran out the door, still dressed in the Merry Widow, the rest of his clothes in his arms. I snatched up the shotgun, emptied both barrels as he passed. He hollered as the blast carried him headfirst into Edna's carriage and the horses bolted, disappearing down the street. I sniffed at the shotgun muzzles, found white powder rimming each crown. Rock salt. The other guy was still alive. His wallet said his name was Liam Griswold, private watchman.

Brrrr.

Nobody was home by the time I'd collected my wits and broken in the front door. Returning through the Sunday-quiet byways of the miniature metropolis, I ducked into alleyways and shadowed niches several times for a change of paratronic identity, each successive alternation a step downward on the ladder of social desirability, from distinguished merchant to anonymous European ship-jumper trying to get underground and stay there.

Then home sweet home. In eighteenth-century Philadelphia, there wasn't such a thing as taking a *room*. My consumer-preferences were at least two centuries unreasonable. I'd have been expected to share a bed with the Boston post-rider, a visiting squad of blue-coats *and* their camp-followers, and an entire family of Polish immigrants who'd never been sanitized for my protection or anybody else's. Business quarters were a house of a different color. It wasn't Holiday Inn; it wasn't even Motel 6. My abode for the duration was an overpriced, rat-infested loft I'd taken over a warehouse for a month's exorbitant advance—good thing damage deposits hadn't been invented—on the seediest back street of an already seedy section of town. They threw in the dry rot, free.

There, musing over "the good old days" of the twenty-second century, I refueled with absent discontent on a day-old loaf of unleavened sawdust and a sausage that belonged in the raw materials bin of a shoe-repair emporium. I'd already transmitted the holos—at a dozen times the real rate taken by my suit—of the latest panicky Market Street get-together and Hamilton's social engagement afterward. I finished by asking Lucy, Ed, and Ochskahrt at one end of the conference-call, and Ooloorie at the other, for comments.

What I got was a non sequitur: "Says here Pennsylvania's the thirty-third largest state in what's gonna be the Union, Winnie, not countin' Quebec. But y'couldn't prove it by the carbuncles on *this* volunteer's backside. I'm gonna talk t'Gallatin about it—I think this here army's marchin' in circles!"

I said, "Don't they all, Lucy?" Ooloorie tried correcting Lucy's geographical misconceptions. I didn't try. Ms. Kropotkin may have been an accomplished individual in her universe, but her knowledge of my own often seemed sketchy.

The last several days had been interesting—like the Chinese curse. In Philadelphia, Washington and Hamilton had prevailed, sending General Light-Horse Harry Lee of Revolutionary fame—ancestor of the fellow who'd wind up leading gray-clad rebels of a different Confederacy—along with fifteen thousand troops in the approximate direction of the dissidents, with instructions to shoot everybody who wouldn't surrender and hang everybody who did. Meanwhile, the buckskin army rolled across the Commonwealth, without regard to formal strategy or tactics, but in full, foolish confidence the antirepublican "enemy" would be swept away, if not by force of arms, then by Jefferson's *Declaration of Independence* and Gallatin's logical extension of it.

The advance elements met in the vicinity of Harrisburg. I wasn't there to enjoy the confrontation in person. By the time Lee's forces and the greater rebel army arrived, I'd already been playing spook-games with Washington and company for a couple of thrill-packed weeks. To be honest, there wasn't much to see. Both sides knew what was about to happen. When the occasion came to pass, somebody hiding behind a nice thick tree waved a white flag.

It was answered by another.

The two flag-wavers met, deep in Penn's Woods, exchanging greetings from their respective leaders. "The General," offered an elderly unshaven junior officer with soiled tunic and tarnished uniform-buttons, "would be pleased to reacquaint himself with Dr. Gallatin, at a place of mutual convenience." By his outfit, he was a member of a Virginia regiment, dirty and tired from his long march to the front, just as the rebels were.

Gallatin's leather-stockinged envoy chuckled. "I am charged, sir, to convey the same message to your commander. These are weighty matters, not to be negotiated lightly. Would you care to step over where we can discuss affairs over a tumbler of what this war is all about?" The unkempt, trail-weary lieutenant laughed. The reluctant warriors shambled through a carpet of last year's leaves toward a pair of bulging saddlebags lying at the base of a tree. The bags were opened. Likewise the gurgling flasks inside. A pause. Another pause.

A question from the officer, wiping his lips: was his opposite number authorized to arrange the time and place in Gallatin's behalf? As he spoke, he displayed signs of dicomfiture, making the rebel representative peer into the woods around them and worry for a moment about the proximity of his pistol.

"Yes, I have that gentleman's warrant and personal confidence. May I inquire as to why you are so ill at ease? Is it the whiskey?" The rebel envoy moved his fingers in a sign known to himself and certain others. Not Masonic. "I assure you," he continued, "I am here by myself, as agreed—nor would I be so impolitic as to ask whether you have also complied with the arrangement."

"Be damned!" exclaimed the stubble-faced officer, returning the sign before he stripped off the faded tunic he was wearing. "This crude deception was not of my creation, and I have bloody well wearied of it! I'm Harry Lee, son, the Devil himself! Now let us decide upon the time and place for this parlay in open fellowship and candor!"

Ed Bear guffawed. As per Gallatin's instructions, he unrolled a fresh copy of the Covenant—intended for conveyance to the general.

"What have you here, son, a request for terms?"

Ed laughed again. Pulling at the flask, the general skimmed the document, then reread it, making *humphing* noises. When he laid the parchment on a knee and took another draft of whiskey, he was silent for a while then said, "The proprietor of Morris House has been explicit, boy—come back with my shield or on it—that damned Illuminatist and his West Indies bastard!" He rose, thrust the parchment in his belt, picked up the abandoned tunic, and swung it over his shoulder. Behind him, the horses shied. "I shall bloody well do neither! Tell Gallatin our convocation should commence immediately—this place will do as well as any—but, tell him, on different terms than stated."

Ed tensed. "Oh?"

"Oh, indeed! Brother, be good enough as to inquire of him what military rank he would afford if I committed to his rebellion. He has a cause here in this seditious paper-scrap I would spend my life defending." With that, the general flung himself over the saddle and galloped out of sight. Gallatin had made his second important conversion, and, like the first, wasn't even there at the time.

The day, and everybody's shoe-leather, wore on.

I'd known Ed for decades. No two individuals were ever closer. Sitting in my loft, with a hint of injury in my tone, I asked about the meeting with General Lee. "Okay, *brother*, what was the funny-business with the fingers?"

"Funny business?" Even a hundred miles away, I could tell his innocence was phony.

"Funny business—you've been in a secret lodge all the time I've known you and never mentioned it? I thought things like that were for the badguys."

I felt him shake his head. "It wouldn't be secret if I told. I can't say more, Win, except... well, most ancient lodges were founded in defense of liberty. It's just that most of them have forgotten. I happen to belong to one that hasn't."

And that was that.

Fortuitously—or not, as Gallatin might have insisted—the converted General Lee tended to the military details after that, without asking Gallatin, or being asked to undertake the task. The same day he met with the philosopher, he gathered his troops about him, read them the Covenant, asked for volunteers to join him in defecting, and sent everybody else home. Those who would go.

One would never go anywhere again. Hearing the first words of the Covenant, he brandished a cutlass-pistol, shouting this was the Devil's work, the end of civilization as we know it, and rushed his commander. The general stood his ground while those around him reacted. There wasn't enough left of the assassin to identify.

The rebel forces, now twelve thousand stronger, and drawing in greater numbers as they passed through the countryside, were becoming more than an army. They were a nation on the march. I watched from my loft as the horde swarmed into the capital, twenty-, thirty-, fifty-thousand strong, unopposed, triumphant, as if it were an ancient Roman procession. Into the heart of the city they marched, me following without much hope of finding Ed and Lucy in the throng, telecommunications or not. A hundred thousand footsteps rattled the buildings. Philadelphia stood weeping and cheering at the curb-sides, waving hats and handkerchiefs, holding children aloft so they could tell *their* children what they'd witnessed this day. Many added their own numbers to the still-swelling mob that overflowed the thoroughfares at every intersection.

Since I knew where they were going, and many of them didn't, I arranged to get there first, recording everything for Ooloorie, following suggestions from the cetacean about camera-angles and lighting. I needed the company, even hers. The government's-eye-view I was getting of the oncoming numbers had even me a bit scared.

At the crest of this human tsunami, Gallatin strode to the portal of Washington's official residence. The crowd hung back, respectful or afraid, as the scholar stepped forward, raised the only weapon he was carrying—his walking-stick—and pounded on the door of the Market Street mansion. There was no immediate answer.

Inside, clinging to military muskets they were afraid to use, the inhabitants cowered at the windows. Hamilton, their real leader, would never be seen again in North America. Gallatin rapped a second time. I'll give this to George: The door swung aside and there, shirt-sleeved, alone, and looking like somebody's maiden aunt in his snowy pageboy, he greeted his rival like an invited guest. Extending a hand, he beckoned Gallatin inside.

"Don'tcha do it, Bertie!" yelled a voice I recognized. I signed off with the twenty-second century, began working across the front of the mob to Lucy. On the porch, the dissident leader stood a while, conversing. Washington nodded, accepted his coat from an unseen aide, stepped onto the walk with Gallatin.

The crowd fell silent. "My friends, the President and I are in agreement. There is but one way to settle this without a bloodbath."

Washington nodded. "Dr. Gallatin and I shall decide the issue between ourselves. Tell me, who will supply the pistols?"

In the confused frenzy that followed, I caught up to Lucy. I had to get back in touch with Ooloorie. This was the old lady's doing. I'd heard her declare it was the only way to fight a war—"*macho a macho*." In my absence, she'd worked on Gallatin. Ed hadn't been any moderating influence. The son of a bitch agreed with her. Grabbing Lucy's shoulder with my left hand, I used my right to key the buttons on my sleeve.

"Ooloorie, we've got a problem—hold still, goddamnit, Lucy. We've got to talk!" She whirled, tears of patriotic joy or something streaming down her wrinkled face. She tried yelling, but there was too much crowd noise. Ed and Ochskahrt were beside her.

"Ooloorie?" No response. With a cold feeling of doom clutching my insides, I tried an alternate frequency, then another, with the same unsatisfying results. "Ooloorie! Come in! I've got to—I can't hear you, Lucy, wait—Ooloorie?"

No answer. Nor would there ever be. My party had been cosmically disconnected. The line was dead, and so were we, stranded in the primitive past. Washington and Gallatin had never fought a duel, not in my universe, not in Lucy's.

We'd destroyed the future.

22
An Ochskahrt in the Works

"Gentlemen, ready your weapons!"

Far away, a drumroll of thunder lumbered through the mountains. There was a loud double *clack!* as two scrolled cocking-pieces were hauled back by their owners till they locked on their respective sears. Silence filled the otherwise empty street.

"At my word, you will step forward," said the referee, some anti-Federalist judge who'd been satisfactory to both parties. "I caution you not to turn, or aim your weapons until you have been commanded to do so!" No one doubted that he meant it: under his judicial cloak he had a modest pistol of his own, double-barreled, twice the size of the antagonists', its unrifled bore stuffed full of powder and carpet nails. "Gentlemen," continued the referee, "since you have refused to reconsider, then upon my signal—and upon my signal alone—you will then level your weapons at one another and discharge them."

In a sense, Gallatin, founder-to-be of the North American Confederacy, faced his arch-rival—not just in politics, but now, it seemed, in metaphysics, as well. President and General George "Father of his Country" Washington towered behind the philosopher in the gloomy thoroughfare, the small of his aristocratic back planted against the stooped shoulder blades of the other, the muzzles of their pistols pointing to the dark and violent sky. In just moments, each would take a walk— ten paces, that was all—and only one was coming back.

It hadn't taken long for arrangements to be made. Composed of battle-scarred and horror-hardened veterans of the recent British unpleasantness—even a few survivors of the French and Indian War (Washington was one of those)—the crowd gathered around Morris House had endorsed the notion of their leaders doing the ducking and flinching for a change. Many had the stumps, hooks, and eye-patches to prove it might have been a good idea a generation earlier. They cleared a space on the pavement. A damp breeze rose, whipping wigs and coattails.

Dueling wouldn't become generally disapproved in my own world for another decade, due to public outrage over a similar exercise between Alexander Hamilton and Aaron Burr. It had never been outlawed in the Confederacy. Cursory reading of history and literature had never quite gotten me over how little most individuals of this period regarded their own lives—

Washington had once written that he found the sensation of bullets whining over his head "charming." And they elected *him* President.

But what surprised me now was that the participants, every combatant, on every side, no matter what they stood to lose or gain, was content to let weighty affairs of principle—to tax or not to tax—rest on the almost random outcome of a smoothbore gunfight between a geriatric general and a gentle but determined schoolteacher.

"Well, boys, we're in for it now," said a voice beside me, speaking of geriatric and determined. I nodded, a sour expression wrinkling my face to match the countenances of my companions. Somehow I knew Lucy wasn't talking about the weather.

Ed shook his head. "Edna had her way, after all, didn't she?"

He was right. Lucy, Ed—yes, even Ochskahrt—and I had come back to prevent just such a thing. Now we stood together, undefeated by our enemies, but beaten by the sheer, stupid force of events. The fact we were marooned in this century, lost forever to our own, wasn't foremost on our minds. Not even mine. I think I'd come to prefer dying to putting things off anymore in the not-quite-death of stasis.

I glanced down at the phony flintlock stretching my belt-leather. The complicated replica wouldn't be of any use to an involuntary pioneer. I'd have to acquire something more authentic. It was growing darker by the moment, now. Lightning flashed, thunder followed.

This whole preposterous disaster was our fault. We'd

bloodied our hands further, negotiating as Gallatin's back-ups. I'd fought a duel once, myself: my six-shot .41 against a customized Luger. A practical people, Americans have always handled these events in a manner disapproved by well-bred Europeans, selecting hardware, loads, and calibers more pragmatic than the expensive toys overcivilized Continentals preferred.

An Anglophile in everything but this, His Imperial Presidency insisted, to keep things even, that he, professional military man and experienced shootist, would stick with half the ornate dueling pair one of his flunkies trotted out in a fancy wooden gift-box. For all the general cared, *Monsieur* Gallatin could use anything short of a howitzer.

It wasn't much short. Wielding powder-flask, ball, and fire-hardened ramrod as if born to it, Lucy helped a sobbing, tear-blinded Cato to charge up Gallatin's choice, one of the enormous horse-pistols he'd brought to Braddock's Field. Not an easy task, filling the flashpan. Not the way the wind was blowing. Ed, Ochskahrt, and I huddled around, trying to give the ordnance team protection. Unlike Washington's genteel piece, Gallatin's had crude but serviceable "iron" sights—a brass bead gleaming over the muzzle in the gathering twilight, a V-notch filed into a section of upturned strap where the breech-piece merged with the woodwork.

In the windswept, cobbled street, dampening with the first tentative dashes of rain, Washington's second opened the parqueted guncase a proprietary crack, allowing the general to make his selection. Ochskahrt beside me, I strode out through the lightning flashes to offer Gallatin's weapon for inspection. Which is how the accident happened.

Thunder *roared*! "Mr. Bear, Herr von Ochskahrt— *look out*!"

I hadn't noticed the loose paving block beneath our feet. Ochskahrt did—the hard way. His toe-tip caught the edge as he passed over it. "Oopsie-daisy—*scheisse*!"

Lightning *flashed*! He lurched. Hollering and flailing, he managed to convert a pratfall into a full-scale avalanche, tripping me so that I fell against the Federalist who, in a futile effort to regain his balance, threw the pistol box into the air. *"Look out for the guns!"*

We were like a row of cursing dominoes. With a shout, the second stumbled against Washington, who, bringing the referee with him, joined us on the wet cobbling at a somewhat lower altitude. Under their newspapers and bedrolls, the crowd roared approval of the brief, unanticipated floor show, Lucy's voice loudest of all. Gallatin remained standing. He looked down at a disheveled heap of men and guns. "Gentlemen," said the Swiss financier. "If you have introduced yourselves to one another..."

That put an end to the formal officiation. There was an embarrassed pause as the audience regained control of itself. With an ill-tempered grunt, Washington heaved himself to his feet, seized a pistol from the broken case Ochskahrt had recovered, checked the pan, and muttered something about getting on with it.

Taking his horse-pistol from where I'd dropped it, Gallatin nodded. That's when the silence started. While

Ochskahrt and I recovered our possessions and got out of the potential field of fire, rejoining Lucy at the curb as she wiped tears of tension-fueled laughter from her eyes, the disgruntled referee swiped imaginary mud off his cloak and began giving instructions. The party was about to start.

"One!" The heavens opened themselves. In the downpour, the two men separated. Not wanting to distract anyone, I refrained from tidying up. I was covered with grit, my nose itched, and, as usual during affairs of gravity, I needed to go to the bathroom.

"Two!" Four torrent-filled yards stretched between Gallatin and Washington. It seemed like forty. The duel I'd fought had been conducted indoors, under rules designed to overcome differences in skill between opponents. In this weather I wasn't sure it mattered.

"Three!" Lucy bit the stem of her pipe in two. She spat out broken pieces, then sheepishly glanced around. She needn't have bothered. No one was watching her.

"Four!" Ed was fidgeting, shifting weight from foot to foot. Well, he had my fingerprints, why not my bladder?

"Five!" I felt a gentle tug on my sleeve, batted the wet, intrusive hand away. The combatants were halfway to the ends of the muddy killing-ground, a soggy ten yards between them. Each carried his flintlock muzzle-upward, pan close to his chest, a hand covering the bore, Washington striding along as if on sunny parade, Gallatin just walking.

"Six!" There was that tug again, insistent. Rainwater streaming down the polished contours of his skull, Ochskahrt was pleading with me through his steamed-up glasses, an expression of distress distorting his features into unrecognizability. Maybe he needed to go to the bathroom, too.

"Eight!" Distracted by Ochskahrt, I'd missed a tick. I frowned at him. He grimaced again, pointing at my middle. I looked down—*oh, no!*

"Nine!"

"Stop!" I heard myself shouting. Gallatin turned.

"Ten!" Both guns went off together, Gallatin's large-caliber *boom!* distinct above the tenor *bang!* of Washington's. Someone's ball whined off the brick wall of a building several yards away. The scene was obscured for several seconds by a cloud of white, evil-smelling smoke. Then the veil was pierced by falling rain and vanished.

Lightning flashing above his head, Washington teetered, a ghastly expression on his face. Twenty yards away, Gallatin let the heavy pistol slip from his fingers, slumped to the pavement, and was still. Washington threw his pistol to the ground. It splashed in a puddle, pivoted on some projection, and came to rest.

The uproar was overwhelming—and it came from human throats. Like the frantic rush to demolish goalposts at the end of a game, the street was filled with people. Quite a few would go home with bruises—one, I'm sure, with a broken arm—owing to my rapid passage among them.

When I got to Gallatin's side, Lucy was already there. "He's gone!" she cried, pointing to the black-edged cavity in the unmoving scholar's shirtfront. Gallatin's legs were crossed at the ankles; his face showed no expression. Already the fatal wound had stopped bleeding.

"Albert Gallatin's dead!" she repeated, as close to hysteria as I'd ever seen her. "That ain't supposed t'happen! He ain't supposed t'die for fifty-eight years!" I opened my mouth—what the hell was there to say?

A grim-faced Cato joined us, along with Ed. The black man had to yell over voices and the weather. "Let's get him outa the street, folks." Cato wasn't crying, now. There wasn't time. The wounded retainer had one more service to perform before he could succumb to grief.

So did I. "Okay, get his feet, Ed. Hirnschlag, get his shoulder, will you? There's something I have to do." I karated my way through the thinning crowd to where the President had stood. His back to me, a souvenir-hunter was bending over the weapon that had been used to kill Gallatin. I kicked upward with every ounce of energy I had. Between his legs. He rose, fell, and lay there, splashing his breakfast on the bricks. I picked up the pistol, inserted a fingernail under the off-side lockplate, and opened it to inspect the lighted dial inside.

I pulled Washington's unfired dueler from my belt where I'd stuck it after the slapstick routine. Waiting for a clap of thunder, I discharged it into an already leaking rain-barrel, then tossed it toward the preoccupied would-be collector. I'd remembered right: Last time I'd used this piece, it had been adjusted to its lowest intensity. Ooloorie and the entire universe might be gone, but, thanks to the fact that it had once existed, fatal bullet-wound or not, Gallatin still had twenty-three minutes to live.

Lightning flashed.

Thunder echoed in its wake.

23

The Big Freeze

I turned the dial as far as it would go.

Slapping the deceptive brass cover back into place, I strode through the rain-soaked street toward my friends where they crouched about the fallen statesman. "Stand back, you guys!"

Lucy and Ed looked up as I pivoted the hammer back. Ochskahrt was overcome with grief and unprepared to notice anything going on around him. I pointed the pistol at Gallatin's head.

"Whatcha think you doin', crazy white man?" Cato seized the pistol, twisting it in my grasp.

"Let him alone, he knows what he's doing!" That was Ed, and he was right. Cato looked at him, then backed off. I reaimed the piece and let the hammer fall.

"This gun got mixed up with Washington's before the duel," I explained, now that I had time. "He's shot—the thing was loaded with a real ball—but the bullet hasn't had time to kill him yet." Thanks to this second dose, Gallatin had twenty-four hours before his wound became a problem. The process could be repeated as long as the batteries held out. And Confederate batteries last a long time.

I tossed the pistol aside and sat down in the mud. Night had fallen, and nobody had noticed. The Rebellion—this one, anyway—was over.

Ochskahrt looked up. "Ve tried. At least ve tried."

"We sure did, Hirnie." Lucy sniffed back tears. There was an odd light in her eyes. I couldn't remember seeing her cry before. She had good reason.

Ed noticed the odd light, too. He rose, leaning on my shoulder. "Win!"

"Now what?"

"Win, I think—"

"Therefore *I* am." I finished for him.

"This ain't no time for clownin'. Lookit what's going on behind you!"

I cranked my head around further. A tiny, brilliant pinpoint had blossomed, giving her eyes the weird gleam I'd thought was incipient senility. A thrill went through me. Wonder spread on Ochskahrt's face. Catching it from us, Cato began laughing.

The pinpoint opened into an azure-edged circle through which an inhuman face was visible. A beautiful, gray, inhuman face. "You landlings had better hurry. I am holding this aperture open across three centuries *and* a tangle of world-lines."

I got up, grabbed the comatose Gallatin by the shoulders. "We're taking him with us! Cato, we're going . . . someplace else. Mr. Gallatin's not dead. If you want to go with us, give me a hand!"

I don't know what the man was thinking about all this, but he grabbed Gallatin's muddy boots and heaved them off the ground.

"Oh no you don't!" I let Gallatin's shoulders back down into the mud. A slim female figure had materialized out of the rain. Edna Janof, still in her kinky outfit, held her laser in one hand. She waved it around, from me to Lucy, from Ed to Ochskahrt. Cato and the fallen Gallatin she ignored. "I'm going through first! Then you're all going to wait here until hell freezes over! I'll blow the machinery on the other side to bits!"

My fingers found the handle of the Rezin. Tickling it out of its scabbard by the guard, I watched Edna as she backed toward the Broach, lifting a foot over its deadly rim. I got hold of the back edge of the Bowie—

And threw!

The heavy blade whipped end over end, burying itself in Edna's abdomen. She stumbled, let the laser fall. The edge cut her in half as she fell through. The Broach never quite collapsed; a muffled explosion spewed parts of her all over the street.

I rose, kicked through the trash, and found my knife. I wiped it off on the tatters of a red-striped shirt and let it slide back into the scabbard.

In the end, we are always alone.

Taking a reluctant last drag on my imported Centaurian cigar, I stubbed it out in a self-cleaning tray and let the couch adjust itself to my contours. In the warm-decorated room, it was *still* cold. I hardly noticed it this time. I was too busy reflecting on what a strange life I'd lived.

In my usual disorganized fashion, I'd witnessed three and a half hundred years of Confederate history, beginning with a scary and spectacular leap right into its middle, in 1987, then living conventionally to the end— mine, not the Confederacy's—finishing with being there at its beginning, apocryphal unauthorized edition though it may have been.

From the looks of things, Albert Gallatin would lead an even stranger life, before he was through. It was confusing to me, let alone an out-of-date philosopher. He wasn't the Gallatin who'd served as Secretary of the Treasury for Jefferson in the universe I came from. He wasn't the Gallatin who'd served as President of the Confederacy. He was a *third* Gallatin who, concerned with principle above all (just like the other two), had died in a duel with an expense-account general in 1794—and been rescued and revivified by time-travelers. In all three cases, he'd contrived to skip the middle of what he'd started. Now he'd have to get used to the fun of living in the latter portion I was doomed to miss.

He'd paid me a visit just before I'd found the door back to the Venus Belt.

"*Mon ami*, they tell me I am living in the twenty-second century." He looked funny in his skinsuit. I'd gotten used to thinking of him in knee-britches. He'd brought other visitors with him.

Lucy was a stranger to this new Earth, as much as

Gallatin and I. She and Ed had been pioneering for decades. Now they'd taken an option on a mining planetoid "where diamonds're big as houses, Winnie!" delighted to be heading back to the endless sky.

Ochskahrt was the happiest of us all. He'd had a rough time. His nerves were gone. He'd stopped by to say his farewells before joining *Tom Paine Maru*— and my daughters in the fleet. They knew their old man, but they were going to be surprised at what he'd been up to this time. With him, I sent my best regards. He planned to go off to a well-established, civilized colony, a planet-of-the-nerds, by-the-nerds, and for-the-nerds. He'd chosen a planet with plenty of closets, no doubt, and no physics laboratories.

Ooloorie was going with him, at least as far as the starship. She was worse than her usual cranky self these days. Growing a new pair of hands will do that to you.

As for us, Clarissa and me, it was more stasis. I hoped that, when they woke us up, they had a cure for freezer-burn.

"Yes, sir," I answered Gallatin at last. "The twenty-second century, and you're responsible for its peace and prosperity."

"That is as it may be, my friend—I must read all of these books I do not recall having written. What if I should find myself disagreeing with them?"

I laughed. Likely he'd take off from the point where an earlier Gallatin had passed away, and cause another two hundred years of revolution. Too bad I'd be missing it. But, with any luck, Clarissa would get better, and we'd jump right into the middle of it again, just as before, and see what he had wrought.

There are worse prospects.

✳ APPENDIX ✳
A Brief Historical Outline*

In 1796 C.E., *the inventive Thomas Jefferson proposed* a new calendar which, at Gallatin's suggestion, employs 1776 as its "Year Zero." Dates preceding the Declaration of Independence continue numbered as before, followed by "C.E." or, where appropriate, "B.C.".

100 Earth-years are equal to 116 Sodde Lydfan, 132 on Vespucci. Scholars are cautioned: ambiguities arise when cataloging events in alternate time-lines (apparently there is only one Confederacy, but many variants of the United States are known), on different planets, or where time-travel is suspected to have been involved.

---

* Compiled from the *Encyclopedia of North America*, TerraNovaCom Channel 485-A, by Edward William Bear of Denver, with permission of the editors.

ca. 3001 B.C.		Sumer. cuneiform writing invented; reports of domest. dogs in Egypt; Yamaguchi W523 exits main sequence; lost Hamiltonian colony estab., Sca.
ca. 948 B.C.		Solomon builds Yahweh Temple, Jerusalem; Attica united by Athen. kings; lost Hamil. col. estab., Obsidia.
ca. 499 B.C.		Pericles born; Tarquinius Superbus defeated by Roman revolutionaries; lost Hamil. col. estab., Vespucci.
ca. 159 B.C.		3rd period of Chin. lit.; water clocks invented, Rome; lost Hamil. col. estab., Hoand; on Sodde Lydfe, death of Martyred Trine begins recorded civilization.

A.L.	C.E.	
-	345	Following death of Constantine, Roman Emp. begins decay; on Sodde Lydfe, Neoned the Aggressor estab. Great Foddu.
-	1592	Nobunaga period, Japan "gives up the gun"; *OMA 789 George Herbert* hijacked by time bandits, Tokyo.
-	1732	George Washington born, Virginia.
-	1743	Thomas Jefferson born, Virginia.
-	1757	Alexander Hamilton born, West Indies.
-	1761	Albert Gallatin born, Switzerland.
0	1776	Declaration of Independence (July 2); Revolution begins.
7	1783	Treaty of Paris (Sept. 3); Revolution ends.
11	1787	Federalists under Hamilton, Jay, Madison, illegally adopt new "Constitution" creating strong central gov't.
12	1788	Ratification by 9th and last necessary state (New Hampshire).
13	1789	Const. in force; Hamilton Sec. of Treasury to G. Washington.
15	1791	Hamilton's Excise Tax passes; angry Penna. farmers rally at Brownsville for beginning of countercoup.
16	1792	Pitts. Convention of antitax forces; Washington issues warning proclamation; farmers tarring and feathering tax collectors.
18	1794	15,000 federal troops ordered against farmers; Albert Gallatin joins rebellion; Washington shot in Phila.; Const. declared

		null and void; Gallatin proclaimed Pres.; Hamilton disappears.
19	1795	Caretaker gov't.; Gallatin declares gen. amnesty; all taxes repealed; property and rights restored to Federalists, Tories.
20	1796	Gallatin confirmed by Cong.; calls for neutral stance between Engl. and Fr., humane Indian policies, Revision of Articles.
21	1797	New Articles ratified with emphasis on civil and economic rights; Northwest Terr. "land certificates" liquidate war debts; gov't. otherwise forbidden to coin or print money.
24	1880	Gallatin reelected (2nd term); Jeffersonian weights and measures.
27	1803	Gallatin and Monroe arrange La. Purchase, borrowing from private sources against value of land.
28	1804	Gallatin reelected (3rd term); Hamilton killed in Pruss. duel; Stevens invents steamboat.
30	1806	Engl. attempts to restrict shipping; Gallatin commissions privateers to defend Amer. vessels.
31	1807	French uphold Amer. sea rights; *Chesapeake* drives off Brit. war vessels; Reverand Forsyth invents percussion firearms; Engl. outlaws slave trade; Jefferson begins anti-slavery crusade.
32	1808	Hundreds of Brit. ships captured or sunk by Amer. private navies, thousands of Engl. seamen desert; 1st ocean-going steamship, *Confederation* (Stevens), sinks Brit. warship; Gallatin reelected (4th term).
35	1811	Jefferson wounded in assass. attempt, kills assailant.
36	1812	Gallatin announces retirement; Edmond Genet elected Pres.
37	1813	Privateers' lawsuit overthrows Doctrine of Sovereign Immunity.
38	1814	Gallatin publ. *Principles of Liberty*, systematic expansion on philosophies of Paine, Jefferson.
39	1815	Privateer Admiral Jean LaFitte publicly denounces slavery.
40	1816	Genet reelected (2nd term), proposes

abolition of slavery, reparatory land-grants
to slaves in West.

41	1817	Slavery abolished for children born after A.L. 44.
42	1818	Gallatin publ. *Rules of Reason*, advoc. nonbinding volunt. legis.; in Engl., Guy Fawkes Day explosion of Parliament believed precip. by Gallatin's works; Brit. gov't. falls.
43	1819	Collier-Shaw percuss. revolver; patent system breaks down under Gallatin's criticism of gov't. enforcement of monopolies.
44	1820	Jefferson elected Pres.; all slavery abolished; Jefferson rejects offers of Presidency for life, threatens resignation.
45	1821	Mexico grants land to Amer. settlers in Texas.
47	1823	Monroe drafts "Jefferson Doctrine": political isolationism, elim. of trade barriers, moral support for colonies asserting "fundamental right to secede."
48	1824	Jefferson reelected (2nd term); internal combustion engine; mechanical calculators; elsewhere, Vesp. Republic estab.
50	1826	Jefferson dies in office; Monroe assumes Presidency.
52	1828	Monroe elected.
54	1829	1st steam railroad (Phila.).
55	1831	Monroe dies in office; John C. Calhoun assumes Presidency.
56	1832	Calhoun elected; Nathan Turner 1st Negro Congressman; Brit. experiments with Gallatinist legislative system; Calhoun's Indian policies denounced by Gallatin.
57	1833	Brit. abolishes slavery, exempts Ireland; Brit. gov't. falls.
59	1835	Colt's double-action revolver; gold discovered in Georgia.
60	1836	Gallatin comeback defeats Calhoun; Tex. declares independence; Santa Anna defeated and killed at San Antonio.
62	1838	Philip and Joseph Webley firearms manufactory, Birmingham, Ala.
64	1840	Gallatin retires again; Sequoyah Guess elected Pres.

65	1841	Mex. declares war on Old U.S., Rep. of Tex.
66	1842	U.S. forces in Mex.; Sequoyah's "Reading" of Gallatin at Buena Vista causes massive Mex. desertions; Mex. City surrenders itself; Sequoyah felled by sniper; Osceola assumes Presidency.
68	1844	Trapper Antoine Janis stakes claim at "Colona" on Cache la Poudre; Osceola elected.
69	1845	Jonathan Browning Arms Co. estab., Nauvoo, Ill.
70	1846	Revolution in Calif.; Hamil. "republic" declared under "Emperor" Joshua Norton.
71	1847	Self-contained cartridges for revolvers.
72	1848	Gold discovered in Calif.; Gal. uprisings throughout Europe; Jeff. Davis elected Pres.
73	1849	Gal. revol. in Canada.
74	1850	Gal. revol. in Mex., China.
75	1851	News of pogroms against Gal. in Calif.; air condit.; Lucille Gallegos born, San Antonio.
76	1852	Gallatin dies; mourning observed throughout world; rumors of celebrations in Pruss., Calif.; Gifford Swansea elected Pres.
79	1855	1st all-steel steamship crosses Atlantic.
80	1856	Arthur Downing elected Pres.
81	1857	Gal. revolt suppressed, India; Brit. gov't. falls.
82	1858	Joint paper on evolution by Darwin, Wallace.
83	1859	John Provost, Antoine Janis, 2 brothers, and their Indian wives form town company at Colona; Downing dies in office; Pres. Harriet Beecher advoc. alcohol ban.
84	1860	Lysander Spooner elected Pres.; Gal. revolts in Ital. states. Chin. Gal. overthrow Hamil. in Calif.
85	1861	Great Northern Pacific railroad begins transcontinental operations, opens extension into Rep. of Calif.
86	1862	Colona settlement renamed "Laporte."
88	1864	Spooner reelected (2nd term); Moray automatic pistol.

89	1865	Actor John Wilkes Booth murdered by obscure Ill. lawyer.
90	1866	Mex., U.S. negotiate Confederation.
91	1867	Elisha Gray invents telephone; smokeless powder; Alaska purchased by Tex. consortium.
92	1868	Spooner reelected (3rd term), proposes Gal. legislature in U.S.; Atlanta-Phila. phone service.
93	1869	Litigation estab. women's vote; Gal. legislature adopted.
95	1871	Great Chicago Fire; official explanation ridiculed in press; predecessor to Griswold's Security founded. *Brrrr*.
96	1872	Spooner reelected (4th term).
99	1875	Electric Street Railway (Chicago).
100	1876	Centennial; Giant "Statue of Gallatin" erected in Lake Mich.; Spooner reelected (5th term).
101	1877	Thorneycroft invents hovercraft; A.G. Bell invents mechanical larynx for chimpanzees.
102	1878	Manhattan "war" between private security companies.
103	1879	Adm./Gen. Wm. Lendrum Mitchell born in U.S. variant and Confed.
104	1880	Spooner retires; Jean-Baptist Huang elected Pres.
108	1884	"Moving pictures" popular; Huang reelected (2nd term).
109	1885	Canada joins U.S.-Mex. negotiations.
110	1886	Geronimo, Mex. national, becomes 1st Congressman to represent others, *not himself*; wireless telephony; simian suffrage.
112	1888	Great Eastern Blizzard; 1st electric. heated streets (Edison); Frederick Douglass elected Pres.
115	1891	1st transatlantic wireless relays betting on Amer. horseraces; Manfred von Richthofen (J.J. Madison) born, Silesia.
116	1892	Benjamin Tucker elected Pres.
117	1893	North Amer. Confed. incl. Alaska, Calif., Canada, Cuba, Mex., Nfld., Old U.S., and Texas; 1st heavier-than-air powered flight (Lillienthal); Brit. Gal. propose Confed. with N. Amer.; Brit. gov't. falls.
120	1896	Tucker reelected (2nd term); dirigible invented.

122	1898	Capt. Forsyth born, Oklahoma City, N.A.C.
124	1900	Amer. capital moved to center of continent; Tucker reelected (3rd term); Hugh Gabbet-Fairfax introduces "Mars" large-cal. automatic—Royal Navy report states "nobody who fired this pistol wanted to fire it again."
125	1901	1st transcontinental aeroplane flight.
127	1903	Dirig. *City of Akron* flies nonstop lngth. of cont. and return; 1st all-talking movie, *Ragtime Dance*, New Orleans.
128	1904	Nicaragua Canal; Tucker reelected (4th term).
130	1906	San Fran. Earthquake, Fire, and Barbecue.
131	1907	Marion Michael ("Mike") Morrison, Confed. movie star, born.
132	1908	Tucker reelected (5th term).
133	1909	1st transatlantic aeroplane; 1st transpacific dirig.; "Sydney Tea Party": all gov't. officials thrown in harbor.
135	1911	Geoffrey Couper, founder of neoImperialist Party, born.
136	1912	Albert Jay Nock elected Pres.
138	1914	Pruss. attacks bordering countries; Continental Cong. declares neutrality; Confed. volunteers launch Thousand Airship Flight.
140	1916	Nock reelected (2nd term); Voltaire Malaise born, St. Joseph, N.A.C.
141	1917	Goddard rockets decimate Pruss. air squadrons; revolt sparked by heavy broadcasting of Gallatin's works.
142	1918	Influenza epidemic; round-the-world dirig. flotilla dispenses exp. vaccine.
143	1919	Edward Bear, father of Edward William Bear, born, April 1, Denver/St. Charles Auraria.
144	1920	Nock reelected (3rd term).
146	1922	Nuclear pile demonstrated (Chicago).
148	1924	Nock reelected (4th term).
151	1927	Television; dolphin communic.; fiss. power (Chic.); Edna Cloud, mother of Edward William Bear, born, Aug. 9, Los Angeles.
152	1928	Cancer linked to malnutrit.; H.L. Mencken elected Pres.; lasers.
153	1929	Fus. power (Detroit); Ooloorie Eckickeck P'wheet born somewhere in Pacif.; Meep

		fam. restaurant chain; heart-lung mach.
156	1932	Jet aeroplane; fus.-powered dirig.; Mencken reelected (2nd term); Olongo Featherstone-Haugh born.
157	1933	Mencken assass.; Continental Cong. chooses F. Chodorov successor; cetaceans join Confed.; heart transplants.
160	1936	Gal. revol. in Spain; Chodorov elected.
161	1937	Artificial satellite launched, southern Mex.
162	1938	Altruistic Protective Enclave of Simians founded, Stanford.
163	1939	Edward William Bear born, May 12, Denver/St. Charles Auraria.
164	1940	Rose Wilder elected Pres.
165	1941	1st simian in orbit reads works of Gallatin, plays chess with porpoises at Emp. Norton Univ. (loses); Hamil. coup in Hawaii; 3-D TV.
168	1944	Wilder reelected (2nd term); F.K. Bertram born, Boston.
169	1945	U.S. atomic bomb destroys Nagasaki; Norrit Gregamer born.
170	1946	T.W. Sanders born, U.S.; Clarissa MacDougall Olson born, Laporte.
172	1948	Wilder reelected (3rd term); limb-regeneration demonstrated.
173	1949	Lunar exped. estab. col.; Dardick open-chamber magazine pistol; laser pistol sights.
174	1950	Jennifer Ann Noble (leader, U.S. Propertarian Party) born, Ithaca, N.Y.; Professional Protectives, Ltd. founded.
176	1952	A. Rand elected, becomes 1st Pres. to travel to Moon.
177	1953	Gal. and Hamil. revol. rock Africa.
178	1954	Jennifer Ann Smythe born (stasis delay), Ithaca, N.A.C.
179	1955	Eugene Guccione invents power cell.
180	1956	Russ. fire on Antarct. colonists; Continental Cong. issues warning; Czar declares war; Rand reelected (2nd term); elsewhere, Communist Reformation begins.
181	1957	Russ. attack Alaska, aid Hamil. in Hawaii, invade Japan; Adm. Heinlein wins decisively at Bering Straits; Russ. suffer huge losses in Antarct. Jap., Hawaii.
182	1958	"Operation Sequoyah": heavy wireless and

		TV, tons of written propaganda employed against Russ. homeland.
183	1959	Lunar col. beam continuous transmissions into Russ.; gov't. collapses, Czar disappears.
184	1960	Hamil. attempt Lunar coup, survivors "spaced"; Robert LeFevre elected Pres.; Neova hovercraft, Securitech Ltd.
186	1962	Hirnschlag von Ochskahrt born in several variants.
188	1964	LeFevre reelected (2nd term); Laporte Paratronics, Ltd. founded; Dora Jayne Thorens born, San Fran.
190	1966	Francis W. Pololo born, Pine Barrens, N.A.C.
192	1968	Mars col., Coprates Canyon; neoImperialist Party founded by Couper; "None Of The Above" wins election.
194	1970	Probability Broach discovered in search for FTL drive.
195	1971	In U.S., D. Nolan Fraser estab. Prop't. Party.
196	1972	John Hospers elected Pres.; Asteroid col. estab., terraforming of Ceres by Harriman, Taggert, and Hill.
197	1973	Cheyenne Power and Climate estab.; 1st stable Broach.
200	1976	Bicent.; Dissolutionist Faction; Hospers reelected (2nd term).
201	1977	Basset coils; 1st "large-sample" Broach.
202	1978	John Jay Madison founds Hamilton Society, Laporte.
203	1979	Hamil. lose final foothold in Uganda; in U.S., S&W M58 discont.
204	1980	Hospers reelected (3rd term); dedication of Pellucidar Gardens, Ceres Central; extrasolar radio signals detected; Turner Vendicom estab.
206	1982	Koko Featherstone-Haugh born.
208	1984	Jennifer A. Smythe elected Pres.; in U.S., anti-abortion terrorists organize "Right to Life Action Squads"; Fed. Security Police (SecPol) quietly estab.; Sino-Russ. confront. results in visible damage to Moon; Dornaus & Dixon begin deliv. Bren Ten.
210	1986	1st contact with human (V. Meiss) on other

side of Broach; G. Howell Nahuatl born.

211	1987	Malaise begins feature series on aster.; Agot Edmoot *Mav* born on Sodde Lydfe; 1st human travels through Broach (E.W. Bear, Denver); Hamil. conspiracy; 7th (and *last*) Continental Cong. convened; systematic Confed. subvers. of U.S. begins.
212	1988	Smythe reelected (2nd term); T.W. Sanders arrives in Confed.; "smartsuits" 1st used in space explor.; neural implants in cephalopods give cetaceans "hands"; unicorns genet. constructed; creation of "Navigation Rock."
213	1989	Malaise transfers news headquarters to Ceres Central.
214	1990	D. Nolan Fraser elected mayor of Denver, U.S.A.
215	1991	In U.S. var., assass. of Blocky Yocks, collapse of Bell System.
216	1992	Olongo Featherstone-Haugh 1st nonhuman Confed. Pres.
217	1993	Construction begins on Laporte Interworld Terminal; hijacked *OMA 789 George Herbert* accidentally arrives in Confed.; mastodons cloned from frozen tissue; plasma weapons.
220	1996	Featherstone-Haugh reelected (2nd term); mass kidnappings of U.S. women first noticed.
223	1999	1st nanoelectronic cortical implants in sapients; Tormount-Malaise conspiracy, secret Hamil. fleet escapes Sol. System.
224	2000	Nomad Clust. aster. 9656 Bester strikes Venus, creating 2nd aster. belt; "None of the Above" wins Confed. election; D. Nolan Fraser elected 1st Propertarian Pres. of U.S.; Lucille Olson-Bear born, Laporte, N.A.C.
225	2001	EdWina Olson-Bear 1st child born (on 1939 Chandler) in Venus Belt, Solar Confed.; quarkotopics.
228	2004	"NOTA" reelected; *Mymysiir* Offe Woom born, Sodde Lydfe.
231	2007	Ochskahrt (U.S.A. variant) discovers time-travel; Ochs. Memorial Academy estab., Tsiolkovsky, Luna; in Confed., "NOTA"